TORTUGA
TRIANGLE

TORTUGA TRIANGLE

BY

THE COMMITTEE

ABSOLUTELY AMAZING eBOOKS

ABSOLUTELY AMAZING eBOOKS

Published by Whiz Bang LLC, 926 Truman Avenue, Key West, Florida 33040, U.S.A.

ISBN 978-1-7330119-9-0

For information contact
Publisher@AbsolutelyAmazingEbooks.com

This book is dedicated to
James "Da Turtle" Hendrick ...

A good man and a good friend.

TORTUGA TRIANGLE

TORTUGA TRIANGLE

A desk is a dangerous place from which to view the world.
                                        - John le Carré

Eight days ago, our United States Coast Guard ship pulled into Port-au-Prince, Haiti, to repatriate another bunch of desperate refugees. Why were people leaving? Why was the U.S. sending them back? Haiti is the poorest country in the northern hemisphere, and it has some stiff competition. It is also a combination of ecological catastrophe, ignorance, cruelty, tyranny and abandoned hope. Columbus described the place as the Garden of Eden. Five hundred years later it was the worst shit hole in the northern hemisphere. Milton must have had Haiti in mind when he wrote Paradise Lost. And the smell. Haiti, once smelled, will never be forgotten. A combination of sun baked shit, garbage, charcoal smoke and triple-distilled despair. That is why people were leaving, and not the usual suspects, young men, but the whole population; pregnant women, small children and the old. Everyone who dared went. Why was the U.S. Coast Guard bringing them back? All of the countries in the area, including the United States, wanted them gone and U.S. Coast Guard were the ones able to do it. Haitians had been killed in normally law-abiding places like the Turks and Caicos and Bahamas. Why? They were poor, black, spoke a strange language, had a different culture and posed an economic threat. The Haitians would do any job at any hazard for whatever pay was offered. The last thing the Caribbean islands needed was a horde of people who could displace them economically. The call went out to Uncle Sam and our uncle sent us.

So, there we were, I didn't like bringing people back to such a place, but we weren't asked. Everyone not on duty

1

got to go into Port-au-Prince if they wanted. Many didn't, which said a lot about the place. Only in Haiti would you be asked if you wanted a telephone and air conditioning. When told that neither worked, the hotel clerk would point to a telephone or air conditioner in your room. The object you wanted was supplied was it not? Whether it worked was beside the point. The same idea applied to every institution in the country. Illusion, not substance, was what was important here. No wonder people resorted to voodoo.

A few of us decided to hit the bar at a hotel that passed for civilization and drown our sorrows. Civilization in Baby Doc era Haiti was defined as electricity, alcohol and non-parasite laden ice. On a good night, the bar scene might include young women from the UN, NGOs or one of the embassies. Americans generally, military particularly, weren't popular with that group, but with local conditions being what they were, a girl sometimes changed her mind.

Tonight was not a good night. Disappointed, but well on the way to coveted inebriation, we were settling the tab, when I looked over and heard two men, one with a Slavic accent and well dressed, the other Latin with too much jewelry for the diplomatic crowd, begin arguing loudly.

"How in hell did you let them get away from you, and how are you going to get them back from Key West?" the Slavic-sounding man ask his partner. "You embarrass me, I kill you. No exceptions. Get them back. Now."

One thing you learn about foreign ports is to keep your nose out of other peoples' business. But it didn't hurt to listen. I was vaguely curious, but my shipmate had more motivation. He was a born-and-bred Conch from Key West. Lavon Perry didn't look very intimidating – heck, in his civilian jeans and Mega-Death T-shirt he could have passed as a Haitian, although his ancestors were actually Jamaicans who had settled in the Florida Keys. He was a distant cousin to Lincoln Theodore Monroe Andrew Perry, better known to 1930s moviegoers as Stepin Fetchit. He liked to brag about it.

Me, I'm a Coast Guard officer from Seattle, red hair,

mustache and perpetual sunburn reflecting my Gaelic forbearers. I don't, and never will, look like a Caribbean islander. Lavon did, and always would. He had no trouble blending in down south and locals opened up to him like they never would to a mainlander. At least, that was my guess as he leaned toward the speakers, picked up a local beer and said, in a deliberate island accent "What are you trying to get back, mon? Maybe I can help."

The Latino reacted to Lavon's offer with undisguised suspicion and a muffled curse. To him, this close-cropped Mutt & Jeff pair in a Haitian bar spelled trouble: maybe military, or worse, DEA. But the Slav shifted his dead-eyed gaze from his partner, toward the skinny stranger two tables away.

"So, you know Key West?" he asked in a half inquiry, half challenge.

"Sure do, born and raised there. Tito Casamayor is my godfather."

The Slav's sunken orbs widened at Lavon's mention of the infamous Detective Lieutenant "Cass," reputed boss of Key West's whores and crooked cops. Pointing to an empty chair at his table, the Slav summoned Lavon to join him and his partner. The invitation didn't appear to include me, but I wasn't about to let a shipmate go into harm's way alone. Following closely behind Lavon, I pulled up a chair and introduced myself by name, rank and ship. More than a few bar brawls in foreign ports had taught me to let the bad guys know up front that backup is available should things begin to get out of hand. The Latin and the Slav looked around. Yes, we had plenty of back-up. And worse, the police and Ton-Ton Macoute, the rightly feared Douvallierist murder squad were under strict orders to leave official Americans alone, the better to impress Washington. If a fight started, the Latin and the Slav would pay, in blood and money. Better to suffer irritating questions than Macoute torture.

Before I could sit down, the Latino's retort was short and to the point: "Private party Gringo!" Checkmate.

My gambit about the ship and crew had failed, so much for the sucker play. I started to open my mouth to speak when the Latino hissed,

"Go back to your sheep Captain Kirk, this conversation is private."

The Slav, who had remained silent up to this point, finally spoke. You should go now my friend, our business is with this one, pointing to Levon. The Latino gave me a greasy smile and nodded his head in agreement.

"Ah, so that's how it is," I snorted, but before my two friends could reply, Lavon broke in pleadingly, "Ahhh Boats!"

"What." I barked.

"Behind you, Now!" was his terrified reply.

I started to turn but it was too late, the big arm had already fallen across my back and I was held fast in a constrictors grip. Only this python spoke French and I was greeted with, "Le Grand Rouge, comment alley-vous."

Grinning like a Cheshire cat, I exclaimed "Boudreaux, Fuzzy Boudreaux!"

There are no rules in bar skirmishes, but one of the finer points is to always keep your eye on your adversary. I therefore turned slowly, to greet my old friend from my days at Station Grand Isle all the while keeping a weather eye on my hosts.

"So Fuzzy, what brings you to Haiti, run out of Tabasco?" Before he could reply, Lavon, with eyes the size of saucepans, inquired, "Boats do we know all these people?"

"*Mon Dieu*, where are my manners?" exclaimed Fuzzy apologetically, "Please to meet my crew."

He gestured expansively at the six men surrounding the table. My smiling gaze about the group was met with hearty laughter and a booming, *"Bonjour, Gran Rouge!"*

It crossed my mind that this group would rather fight than drink, so time was of the essence.

I gestured to the Slav, may we take a seat? He fixed me with an impassive face, looked over towards the Latino

4

shifting uneasily in his chair, then back at me. With his right hand he motioned for all to take a seat. As I took the chair, my instincts told me that this guy was no amateur; he was a professional. But a professional what? Since meaningful conversation was probably not going to take place under these conditions, a thirsty consensus formed, and with a great scraping of tables and chairs the gang of unlikely characters gathered to, " Get shit-faced in a circle," which is also a custom in many ports.

Lavon sat quietly with his mouth open as Boudreaux and the boys formed a loose circle around the table. Twitching like a rooster before cockfight the Latino looked for a means of escape while the Slav's hooded eyes got hoodier and his cruel mouth drew tight.

While everyone was adjusting themselves so they could drink without interruption, I leaned towards Lavon, "Cozy, huh?"

"What's going on here Boats, I thought we just came for a couple drinks."

"We did, until you opened your mouth and butted into somebody else's business. Why did you do it?"

"I don't know, man, I'm going stir crazy down here, I want to talk to somebody besides the same bunch of dipsticks every day. I think I'm getting tired of other people's problems, especially on this rock, where we are swept by the wind of a thousand sorrows.

Lavon was a bit of a poet.

"So now I'm a dipstick?"

"Not really, you know what I mean Boats, don't you. I just want a life, a life I'm in charge of.

"Yes, well good luck."

A second round of drinks arrived. It had only been ten minutes since the first.

I noticed the Slav eyeballing the Latino who seemed to get drunker with each passing moment. The scent of cigarettes, whiskey, beer, commissary perfume and cigars filled the room. The last glass on the tray, a glass of iced tea with a tea bag still inside, was delivered to the Slav. A

5

dangling paper tea-tab on the outside of his glass read, *HIMALL-YAN.*

In my experience anyone who drinks tea, especially HI-MALL-YAN tea with Haitian ice, is a highly suspicious character. That is why I force myself to drink rum instead of tea, to keep up appearances.

However, still trying to follow my own advice, I kept my mouth shut and waited for the show to begin. There was no way Boudreaux would waste a night being sober and pain free. Across the room a local stage band was giving voice to an apparently popular native song:

"Gotta go on down to Zombie town,
where death is overrated.
I'm sure I see you der' too,
once de soul has been deflated."

After a series of friendly threats and exaggerations everyone settled into their drinking. The Slav turned towards me. "I do not know who you are, but I believe you have made very big beef steak."

I was flattered, but said, "You mean miss-take?"

"Oh, yes, miss-take, sorry, English not so good. Ha ha! "

"Well, I don't know who you are either, nor do I give a flying military *Kurva*, but whatever my miss-take is, it's well supported. Look around."

The Slav seemed surprised by my use of the Czech word for shit. He turned slowly and reviewed Boudreaux and company. Did he think these guys were my Coast Guard crewmembers? His eyes were now fully hooded like an old VW Beetle, so he couldn't see much, but his grim Slavic lips formed a thin black line like a Boston Blackie moustache in the wrong place.

I asked. "Look pal, we just came for a drink, my friend got a little curious when he heard the words, Key West, but that's all there is to it. And, if you'll forgive me saying," I glanced around, "You look like you're very well prepared for the past, but for the future ... eh ... not so much."

The Slav blinked, *"Pako!"* (Czech word for dork.)

"You're a big meanie," the Latino suddenly spouted and

6

pointed at the Slav, then sucked down his second double rum and looked up like he'd just found his balls.

"Okay, Senor *Le Grand Rouge*, here eez dee deal," the Latino turned toward me.

The Slav reached to stop him, but Boudreaux, who enjoyed party favors, hooked his finger in the back of the Slav's shirt and lifted him off the chair. Poor fellow looked like a *marionette* with only one string. Boudreaux winked at me and I knew the fun was about to begin.

"Paloma que falta! Paloma que falta!" the Latino suddenly cried and flapped his arms. The words hung in the air like the howl of an urban wolf, wailing from a high-rise condominium balcony.

The Slav seemed embarrassed by the outburst and reached for his wallet. He flipped a big wad of some type of currency on the table then got up, nodded to the group and left with the Latino in tow.

I pushed back and noticed a cheap, mildewed business card had fallen out of the stranger's wallet. I picked it up.

Jimmy Da Turtle
Terrapin Law
1 Shell Tower - Ground Floor
Key West, Earth

I fix things.

I left the business card on the table. Strange. I knew a lot of lawyers. Some could be described as bottom feeding slime-ridden filth, some as weasels, and some even made the jump to human status, but none reminded me of a "Da Turtle." I didn't know of any Da Turtles who needed a lawyer either, so I forgot about the card and remembered why I had come to a bar in the first place. I came to drink and resumed doing so, along with the rest of our newfound friends who had never forgotten and had been pulling ahead in the last few moments.

Most of the conversation consisted of grunts, half-laughter and cries for another round, but finally Fuzzy asked Lavon what in the hell a Paloma was.

"It's a Pigeon," was his reply.

"Can't be, all the pigeons in Haiti were eaten years ago, it must mean something else," was Fuzzy's retort.

"You want a history of birds in this Third-World paradise, get a copy of the *National Geographic*. I know what I heard, and what he said was Spanish for pigeon." Lavon crossed his arms on his chest.

This clever repartee rapidly descended into, "Your mother swims out to meet troop ships – your mother stowed away on troop ships," and it looked like things might be headed toward the parking lot. These guys have a future as political speechwriters, I thought, while the rest of the table tried to prevent a fight.

Then things stopped. Cold. I could have sworn that I saw ghostly images rising from the floor. Even gravity stopped and for good reason.

There are dresses, and then there are dresses. She was wearing the second kind.

She didn't walk; she glided to our table. We stared so hard we started sweating.

"Good evening, gentlemen," she said in perfect, but French accented, English. She was tall, with long black hair and perfect Polynesian features. It only took a glance around to realize she was talking to us by default, the rest of the crowd being even further down the evolutionary scale than we were.

"What's a nice girl like you doing in a place like this?" Lavon finally managed to stammer.

She flashed a million megawatt smile, "Nice? *Pas moi.* Still, I was hoping you could help me, I am looking for a well-dressed Slavic man and a scruffy looking Cuban. Have you seen them?"

Meanwhile, I was thinking that this was some sort of alcohol-induced remake of the *Maltese Falcon*. Did either of those two clowns look like Peter Lorre or Sidney Greenstreet?

8

"As fate would have it, they left ten minutes ago" I replied, still stunned by her. She was obviously the most beautiful woman on this planet and probably several others. "They don't look like your type, what could you possibly want with them?"

"They aren't my type, they're Pica and I am Elite," she replied, "but I still want to talk to them. Did they mention pigeons, by any chance?"

Then she saw the abandoned business card and her eyes flashed dangerously.

"*Mon Dieu*, Da Turtle ! That horrible, fiendish little man. This will be the end of International Pigeon racing as we have come to know it. Excuse me; I must call my editor at once."

"Wait," I said. "Who are you?"

I wasn't about to let her get away without knowing more. Beautiful Polynesians with a French accent have always been a fantasy – actually, a wet dream – of mine. One of the reasons I'd joined the Coast Guard was the aim of going to Bali or Bora Bora or Tahiti and meeting some of those exotic women painted by Gauguin. But instead of Indonesia or the South Pacific, here I was in Haiti, the asshole of the world. Bad luck had followed my career and the assignments proved to be a chart to nowhere.

The woman paused, looking back at me. Her eyes were like black pearls, reflecting the twinkling lights behind the bar.

"*Moi*? My name is Moana Jones, I work for the *International Herald Tribune*."

"Ah, that explains the French accent. That paper's based in Paris," I said, showing off my powers of deduction. Sherlock Holmes in a Coast Guard's uniform.

She shook her head, making the raven-black hair sway like one of those hula dancers you set on a car's dashboard.

"True, the newspaper's home office is in Paris. But my way of speaking came with me from French Polynesia. I was born on Moorea. That's part of the Windward Islands, just north of Tahiti."

"Moorea?" I repeated dumbly.

"It means Yellow Lizard. We have a few."

"And your name – what does it mean?"

"Jones ?"

"No, Moana."

"It means Ocean," she smiled.

"Perfect," I nodded. I thought I might be in love.

"I have to go," she said. "I'm supposed to interview those men about the pigeon races. But Da Turtle – he's a wild card I didn't expect. This ruins everything."

"But – "

Before I could finish the sentence she was gone. Suddenly the bar, despite its hordes of rowdy patrons, felt empty.

"Smooth move," said Lavon. "You let her get away."

I stared at the still swinging door. A whiff of her perfume lingered in the air and reminded me of the ocean on a clear night.

"I'll find her again," I said. "All I have to do is find the Slav and his pal."

"Or Da Turtle ," Lavon reminded me.

I stared down at the business card. *I fix things* – what did that mean?

~ ~ ~

For some, alcohol acts like a poisonous amplifier, each round twisting the nastiness knob exponentially to the right. For me, it's more like fuel; a few shots to top off the tank, and I'm good for whatever the evening brings. But there's a point at which even the largest tank begins to overflow, and after an evening of drinking, that point was well behind me, receding like a Caution sign in the rear-view mirror of a speeding car.

Staring into my empty glass and bemoaning Moana's departure, it took me a few minutes to absorb Lavon's mention of Da Turtle . Peering through the alcoholic fog clouding my mind, I struggled to get a clear view of the evening's events. Something about a missing pigeon, or was it pigeons? The Slav's demand to get "them" back, and

Moana's inquiry about racing pigeons, didn't match with the Latino's exclamation about a "Paloma," which even my addled brain recognized as a singular noun. Were they speaking in code? Perhaps "pigeon racing" meant something less civilized than the tradition-laden sport of racing *Voyageurs*. A Haitian bar certainly seemed an odd venue for a gathering of pigeon fanciers.

Of the two people who might hold the key to this puzzle, one was a Herald Tribune reporter, and the other a reputedly ruthless lawyer. An easy choice: *cherchez la femme*, but where to begin looking?

The stench of stale smoke and boozy breath dissipated as I stepped out into the sultry tropical air. If I had the nose of a bloodhound, the lingering scent of Moana's perfume might have led me to her, but the only exceptional feature of my nose was its ruddy prominence, so I had to rely instead on my somewhat diminished reasoning ability, a dangerous practice in a seedy foreign port. Hmmm....if I were traveling on a Herald-Trib expense account, where would I stay? The answer suddenly appeared as obvious as the nose on my face: up the hill, in the comparative comfort of *Petionville, the mansion infested home of the local elite.* Lavon, who had followed me out of the bar, was quick to offer a suggestion:

"I'll bet the travel agent booked her a room at the Karibe." Lacking any better lead and feeling a deep thirst returning, I hailed a taxi and we set out in search of Moana.

The Karibe was no Ritz Carlton, or even a Best Western, but it was the best that *Petionville* had to offer, which meant canopied beds, functioning ceiling fans and hardly any dead rats. Oh, and an outdoor bar, a logical point to begin inquiring into the whereabouts of a stunning Polynesian woman. The bar was quiet, deserted except for a white-jacketed bartender and an impassive-faced gringo in a mildewed linen suit. Lavon recognized the gringo immediately.

"Da Turtle !" he exclaimed.

Hearing his name invoked, Da Turtle cast a

noncommittal glance our way. I could see at once why he had been given that moniker. Nothing in his demeanor betrayed the slightest hint of what might be going on in that oversized head.

My pulse quickened as my expectations soared. "Nice piece of detection, Sherlock," I said, glancing at Lavon. Da Turtle had turned away and now appeared preoccupied with his brandy snifter.

The white-jacketed bartender motioned for the two of us to take a seat at the table adjacent to a large fichus tree. I was about to protest, when Lavon grabbed my arm and deftly slid me into a chair at the aforementioned table. The top of which had not seen a cleaning cloth in quite some time, but it did offer an unobstructed view of my quarry, Da Turtle.

Lavon, after seating me, moved around to the other chair and after noisily seating himself, flashed a board grin and pronounced "Ain't dis real nice." "What's so nice about it" I snapped back at Lavon. "There are about twenty feet between me and that Da Turtle friend of yours, and I desperately want to have a conversation with him, to find out what he knows about Moana."

Lavon gave a short laugh, looked skyward and said," That ain't gonna happen."

"Says you," I shot back." I was about to rise, when the bartender arrived and inquired in perfect Queens English, "What can I serve you two gentlemen?" Without hesitation I blurted out, "what he's drinking," pointing in the direction of Da Turtle . "Alas sir I cannot accommodate you, the gentleman across the room is drinking from private stock." "I can offer you a very nice house brandy, if you are so inclined in that direction?"

"Yeah, that's fine," I replied, "Two house brandies, one for me and one for my friend."

The waiter smiled, nodded, then headed back in the direction of the bar. After he was out of earshot, I turned to look at Lavon,

"He ain't gonna talk to you," Lavon laughed.

12

"Why not," I queried?"

"Cause you need to be introduced to him, that's why not."

"What do you mean introduced, don't you know him? So introduce me," I shot back to Lavon. His reply was simple and to the point, "You gotta show conversation money or maybe you have something he wants, otherwise forget it."

Feeling a bit like Faust, my reply was, "I would trade my soul for that woman right now!"

The oversized head turned in our direction upon hearing my declaration, and I knew at that instant that I was face to face with Mephistopheles.

Our drinks were delivered by a white jacketed waiter. The letters DMD were embroidered on the breast pocket. Before I could inquire as to why a waiter had a monogramed jacket, the skinny British ex-pat, whose outfit also included jodhpurs and steel-toed flip-flops set our drinks upon the table.

"Stiff upper lip and all that rot, Chappie's," he said, then slapped at a fly on the sticky table top and departed. As he turned, I noticed back of his starched jacket also displayed another large monogram, DMD, positioned above crossed cricket bats with goat scrotum device. Interesting.

I elevated my snifter nose-ward in a casual toast to Lavon and a sideways tip towards Da Turtle . The terrapinish man responded with a slight bobble-headed nod, while his eyes and mouth remained impassive. Do Turtles have lips, I wondered, but not wanting to waste this opportunity to speak with him, I stood and looked at Lavon.

"OK, Red Rider, (he liked it when I called him Red Rider) if you won't help me I guess I'll have to do it myself."

With a deep inhalation and another full slug of brandy, I turned to face Da Turtle.

He was gone.

I moved briskly across the shadowed patio and tried to remember exactly which table was his. Stopped when I thought I'd found it. Only a small piece of paper remained, held fast under a bottle of *Nap Boule'!* hot sauce. A precise handwritten message, inscribed on a single perforated sheet of 3-ply, third-world toilet paper read, "You like pussy?"

Did I have the right table? Surely Da Turtle couldn't read my mind. Surely he would have a higher calling, a deeper insight into the working of a manly man's mind than to suggest something so wonderfully tawdry.

For a moment, as you might imagine, I was disturbed by such blatant crudeness, but quickly grasped the genius of the large-domed man who, without a spoken word already knew far more about me than I was willing to admit, even to myself. He was an agent of Lucifer, indeed. I read it again. I felt dizzy, then something reminded me of something else that remin.... I turned towards my table. The drinks were catching up, my tanketh overfloweth.

A gunshot rang out, someone farted and I was pulled aggressively to the deck by a man dressed all in black. He leaned close to my face, a tortured black cocktail straw clenched between his perfect gums, "I can get you published for less than the cost of a good piece of ass, plus bookmarks, made in China! Lord Gorton Pimlico Blackstraw at your service, old bean."

Although the suggestion had some merit, I was a slave to due diligence and had not priced ass recently for comparative analysis. I shook myself loose from the seedy fellow, and then stood to see what was going on.

In so doing, I amiably provided a large, convenient, white-assed target for anyone interested. The patio was almost deserted when I caught a glimpse of someone moving gracefully into the night.

"Whoa, hold your horses, Red Rider, that's Moana!" I looked wildly for Lavon.

I found him. Slumped in his chair, a small caliber bullet hole between his non-seeing brown eyes, Lavon was dead. His skinny black legs twitched in the hideous gavotte of death, musical heritage perhaps, and on our table a single white feather floated in my half-empty brandy snifter.

"Fuck. Not that damn *La Paloma* bird shit again," I

groaned and unintentionally harmonized with the sounds of the oncoming *Police Nationale* sirens.

~ ~ ~

Lavon Perry. Dead. Until now, this miserable evening was just that. Miserable, but no worse. Now it was a damn tragedy. A family had lost a son. The Coast Guard had lost a good man. I had lost a good friend. For what? Pigeons? Pigeons? I had to tell his parents that their son had died because of some God damned pigeons. This was a bad joke and I'd be damned if his death certificate read "cause of death – bad joke." I had to find out what was going on for his sake if for no other reason.

In the meantime here came the police. Lots of sound and fury – they had already gathered up whoever was in the parking lot and were beating the hell out of any Haitian dumb enough to be found there and were being unctuous to any European. No sign of managing a crime scene. At least that is what I was thinking until I caught sight of Police Commandant Rene Crevecoeur. Tailored uniform. Sun glasses that would be the envy of a jazz musician. Same "seen it all and don't give a damn" expression. He was the second son of the Minister of Justice so he really didn't have to give a damn. Except, in his spare time, he did. He was actually a first-class cop when the mood struck him. We knew each other from an FBI course that we had taken a couple of years ago. Rene had been sent as one of Haiti's good-will gestures designed to show a few steps toward progress that would impress Washington and get the American do-gooders off of official Haitian backs. It turned out that Rene was actually interested, and showed a brilliant aptitude for investigative police work, when it suited him. I just lost a friend and wanted to see if I could shake off Crevecoeur's sense of detachment long enough for him to do some real police work. We caught sight of each other and he looked over at me.

"Thanks for ruining a perfectly good evening," he said. "I was headed up to Pationville to spend time with my, ah, niece, when I got the call. Nice to see you, except that it

15

isn't. No rest for the weary. You know the deceased?"

"Yes, he was a friend of mine and a member of my crew. Can you help find out who did this?"

"Of course I can – the question is, will I," Crevecoeur responded. "A pack of white mice teaching us the benefits of civilization, well, white except for this one. Frankly, someone may have done the people of Haiti a favor."

"Go to hell," I responded.

"You need to check your geography, this is about as close to hell as you are likely to get. You visit, I live here, at least until I can do some creative banking and move to Paris. You say corruption; I say an ancestral piece of the action. This is the family business you know. Just for grins, ditch the moral rectitude and pitch in now that I'm here. What happened?"

I filled Crevecoeur in on our meeting, the Slav, the Cuban, and Da Turtle.

While I was filling Crevecoeur in on the details another car pulled up. It was the RSO – Regional Security Officer – from the embassy. You didn't get assigned to Haiti for perfect performance. Not even for perfect attendance. This was a hardship tour, and no one was more hard-up than Smith, the RSO. The problem was that Smith was good, really good. He had either pissed God himself off or wasn't who he said he was. The jury was out on that one but I was still glad to see him. So, strangely, was Crevecoeur, who normally didn't like anyone outside his immediate social circle, especially middle-aged white guys.

"Hey, Rene, you going to keep up the gratuitous brutality or have your guys do something useful," Smith growled.

"Just keeping up appearances, you have to give the people what they want," Crevecoeur replied. "Just what I needed, a visit from the ACLU. Actually, we have recovered a shell casing, got a description of the possible shooter and a description of the car she used. Not bad for a crew from the third-world If I say so myself. Oh, but I'm supposed to be humble."

"Did you say, she?" I asked.

"One of us needs to learn to understand English," Crevecoeur replied. "We didn't get much of a description, but we know the shooter was a woman, who apparently is fond of silenced .22 pistols. Which reminds me, weren't you sitting in that chair?." You can't tell me she couldn't tell the difference between a skinny black kid and a headed-for-cancer white guy. He was shot for a reason. What that reason was, I intend to find out. It offends my sense of order."

That is when I had to leave. I left the hotel and got back to the ship. I had to inform HQ of Lavon's death, tell the crew what happened and somehow tell Levon's parents what had happened. This was my sixth pass at being the Angel of Death and it never got any easier, especially when you were almost a member of the family. Smith offered up the embassy car to get me back to the ship. I accepted. Just as I was getting in I heard Smith and Crevecoeur talking.

"Rene," Smith asked, "do you truly know what is wrong with the Third-World?"

"Do tell," Crevecoeur replied.

"It is that just a few dollars can buy a lot of protection – no offence."

"None taken," said Crevecoeur, "but the tariff is so high in that valley that even I can't go there, and I am supposed to be running the place. Something serious is going on over there with these damn pigeons. Shooting a few of my people is bad enough, but they must think they are invulnerable if they think they can shoot an American and no one can touch them ..."

From the Key West Citizen:

"Petty Officer First Class Levon J. Perry. U.S.CG, died in the line of duty in Port au Prince, Haiti, on August 1, 1983. Petty Officer Perry was an eight year veteran of the Coast Guard. Petty Officer Perry was a native of Key West, a graduate of Key West High School and Florida Keys Community College. He is survived by his parents, Levon Perry Sr. and Grace Perry. He is rich in the love of his family, the respect of his friends and shipmates and the thanks of his country. Rest in Peace.

~ ~ ~

Marie Lavoisier was eating a pigeon. What good fortune, she thought. This bird was much tastier than the sinewy, hardscrabble chickens she sometimes caught. But what was a pigeon doing in these parts? Surely they had all been hunted to extinction on this portion of the island. People went hungry in this neighborhood. She could hardly believe it when the fat-breasted bird landed on her window ceil. Bad luck for the budgie. Dinner for Marie.

Only twenty-two, she was a beautiful woman, her skin the color of strong coffee. This indicated that she was a Haitian from the interior where bloodlines were less diluted. Her breasts were high and rounded; her hips curvy. But, men feared Marie rather than desired her, an unfortunate consequence of her trade.

"*Apporte-moi les* Heinz?" Marie called to her mother. Ketchup would give the roasted bird more flavor. But the old woman waved her away, saying, "*Nous en avons pas.*" There was no such condiment to be found in this 16-by-20-foot shack that served as a *hounfour* temple. Foodstuff was usually provided by Marie's followers, but business had been slow lately. Things usually shut down when the U.S. Coast Guard was in port. People were afraid to show their true beliefs around these armed white foreigners.

Most people hereabout knew Marie Lavoisier was a servant of the spirits, a *mambo*. She had been chosen for this position when only fifteen, selected by her dead ancestors while in a state of possession. What the local *hounsis* had taken for a devout state was actually more medical than spiritual. Marie had suffered from epilepsy since childhood.

As a *mambo,* it was her responsibility to preserve the sacred rituals, the *Priyè Gine* and songs, as well as maintain the relationship between the spirits and her community. She'd moved with her mother to this far-flung neighborhood of Port-au-Price as a child.

She kept her voodoo paraphernalia stored in a box under her bed. In addition to a colorful ceremonial suit, she made use of a bell and her *asson*, a calabash rattle containing stones and snake vertebrae.

Marie would be using these tools of her trade tonight, for she had been asked to revive the dead. To live again usually took a year and a day, but sometimes she could call on Dark Spirits to intercede. She knew it would take a more powerful *loa* than Damballa, the Sky Father. Damballa had created primordial life, but bringing back the dead required a *baka*, a malevolent spirit sometimes found in animals. Eating the pigeon might give her access to such a force.

This ritual was usually performed by a *bokor*, but she was being paid a large sum of money by someone known as Da Turtle to resurrect a dead man, an American sailor named Lavon Perry. It was a very tricky process, for if she failed, the *ti bon ange*, a portion of his soul, would escape the body, leaving him as a zombie.

Being very cheap, Da Turtle would not pay her for delivering half a man.

~ ~ ~

To the Slav, it seemed much longer than two days since he had phoned Key West to engage Da Turtle's services. In the course of a decade spent slinking about the Caribbean in disreputable pursuits, the Slav had often heard the expat dictum that time passes more slowly the closer one gets to the Equator. But latitude alone couldn't explain why Haiti felt far more than a time zone or two South of the real world. "This devil island," as he had come to refer to Haiti, was a purgatory where clocks seemed to run backward, and nothing much else ran at all. Now, despite the ample retainer that the Slav had wired to Key West in order to expedite Da Turtle's arrival in Port-au-Prince, the wily lawyer appeared to be in no hurry to resolve the matter for which he had been retained.

"I hire you to fix pigeon problem, not raise dead man," protested the Slav.

"Indeed," replied the taciturn lawyer; "Sudden violent

19

death has a way of changing things." That ironic retort, unaccompanied by any discernible facial expression, reduced his client to sputtering apoplexy. Averting the torrent of threats and Slavic curses that would have followed shortly, Da Turtle continued: "We find the killer, we find the birds."

Without further explanation to his bewildered client, he rose from his seat in the Karibe's lobby and walked outside, where a nondescript white sedan waited at the curb. "Rene!" he exclaimed, embracing the uniformed PNH officer who stepped out to greet him. A fleeting smile crossed Da Turtle face and was reflected on Crevecoeur's sliver-mirrored sunglasses.

Police Commandant Rene Crevecoeur had first met Da Turtle a few years before, when the lawyer appeared in Port-au-Prince to represent the crew of a Key West-based schooner wrecked during Hurricane David. Given the clandestine nature of the ship's cargo, successfully negotiating its recovery and the crew's safe release required exceptional negotiating skills....and even better connections with the PHN, Haiti's national police force. Having concluded that matter to the mutual satisfaction and profit of the PHN and the entrepreneurial seafarers, Crevecoeur and Da Turtle enjoyed each other's trust and respect. So, Da Turtle knew whom to turn to for help when he received a cryptic call about pigeons having flown the coop in Haiti. And now the two had another mystery to solve: the murder of my friend Lavon.

Basic crime scene investigation coupled with a crude but effective interrogation technique had provided Police Commandant Crevecoeur some leads to follow, but his best eyewitness was laying on a bar floor with a bullet in his forehead. In most places, that would rule out getting a statement from the victim, but this wasn't most places. No, this was Haiti, where black magic reputedly could restore full conversational ability to the dead. If the *voodoo* ritual succeeded, Lavon could soon be chattering with the verbal velocity of a morning talk-show host.

It hadn't taken Da Turtle long to figure out that the murder and the pigeon theft were somehow linked, so he was quick to provide the cash that Crevecoeur said would be needed to hire the best young talent in the local reanimation business: Marie Lavoisier. She was reluctant to accept the assignment. Having no experience as a *bokor*, and fearful of angering the sinister-looking white man should she fail, Marie at first declined the tendered payment. But the Police Commandant was persuasive, and the fortunate appearance of a fat pigeon on her windowsill signaled encouragement from the spirit world. Sinking her teeth into the bird's roasted flesh, she invoked the *baka*.

~ ~ ~

Ten kilometers, as the crow crawls, Key West attorney, Da Turtle and Crevecoeur exchanged a few pleasantries, spoke of the weather in France, for each man had a penchant for fine wine. Shortly, having gleaned no useful informaon, Da Turtle bid Rene, *au revoir,* and headed off in the direction of his favorite bistro. Da y being pleasant, the walk being short and through the best section of the city, the attorney at law arrived at his destination with a sense of great expectations.

Just past two in the afternoon the placard in the doorway announced closed, but the door opened and as was his custom entered and seated himself. "Hayee no sitting, we are closed!" A waiter shouted in the direction of the unwanted dinner. The large head moved deliberately around to face the sound of this unpleasantness. "Ahh pardon, *Monsieur Tortue*," apologized the truculent minion. Da Turtle turned back to his menu and his thoughts.

The morning had gone off rather well and he found himself in a somewhat jovial mood. Events could not be progressing better and he felt intoxicated with the dubious felicity of success. The only dark cloud in this grand gest was the *Bokor*, Marie Lavoisier, a mountebank clearly out of her depth. The cognoscenti harbored a particular distain for the amateur and only consented to her use upon the glowing recommendation of Rene. Clearly Rene desires a tryst at some future date, he smiled to himself. His reverie was broken by the sound of a familiar mellifluous voice. *"Mon bon ami, bon ami,"* exclaimed Email Diamanté, proprietor of the Bistro International.

"Bonjour" ejaculated Da Turtle with great delight.

Da Turtle, whose real name was known only to a few law enforcement agencies and great number of massage parlor owners, was justifiably paranoid about current communication technology. He had lived too long in the tropics to ever completely trust anyone, or anything, including himself.

After a few glasses of *Campari,* Email Diamante' led Da Turtle up a small staircase, (Da Turtle did not like stairs,) and onto the dark rooftop of the *Bistro International.*

Laid out neatly on a small table were a yellow fountain pen and two tiny sheets of thin, blue, Zig Zag rolling papers. With a handful of cash and a nod, Da Turtle dismissed Email and sat down to write words that might, if properly phrased, change his position on the food chain.

After carefully lettering two identical messages, he rolled the papers tightly and inserted them into small aluminum tubes. He knew that a carrier pigeon flight this long would be dangerous and it would be better to have two chances for success, rather than one. When he finished, Da Turtle stomped his foot three times on the tin shingled roof top. Email reappeared, took the tubes and walked across the gable to a large, square cage draped with a yellowed bed sheet.

Da Turtle stood, pocketed the pen and turned away. He was thankful his friend Miguel Santoro, back in Key West, had completed this mission and delivered to him a most secure means of delivering a message of great importance. Da Turtle mumbled an old pirate dirge that he was fond of repeating, "The onliest man ye can trust is a dead man, for it's he who'll tell no tales."

As Email pulled the tangled shroud off the rusty

chicken wire cage, he observed only one bird remained and turned quickly to advise Da Turtle . Had Da Turtle remained vigilant, instead of entertaining himself with old pirate philosophy, he also would have noticed there was only one bird in the cage. But it was too late, Da Turtle was gone.

Email gently strapped the remaining silver tube to the pigeon's leg then tossed the bird into the dark night air. The unused message pod was tossed off the roof and into the fetid alley below. Email pulled the shroud over the cage and after a quick look at the sky, descended the rickety wooden stairs.

~ ~ ~

Two hours before midnight, a singular pigeon named, Little Binky, climbed into the smoky voodoo sky above Port au Prince, circled once then headed northwest and winged resolutely towards the far-off island of Key West. She was alone and missed her flying companion, another carrier pigeon named, Mahvalis. Mahvalis, who had mysteriously disappeared the day before after flying out of their rooftop cage to take a shit on some tourists. Mahvalis had said she was bored.

Mahvalis and Binky had arrived in Port au Prince a few days earlier, smuggled in aboard an old sailing schooner out of Key West named, The Wolf. The Wolf dropped anchor in Port au Prince Bay and according to the captain, had arrived to assist in a "humanitarian relief" effort.

Little Binky and Mahvalis, both famous in pigeon racing circles, had endured ten days of rum talk, cheap bird seed and marijuana smoke while hanging in a guano-filled cage displayed in the captain's cabin. Racing pigeons only fly in one direction-back to their loft and Little Binky knew from previous adventures that the trip out was usually much worse than the trip back.

The tropical sea salted air embraced Binky as the white bird automatically corrected her aerodynamic posture to compensate for the small tube affixed to her right leg and quickly determined the most favorable altitude for flight.

23

Winds at the surface were light and from the southwest. Binky loved the following wind on her feathered butt and fluffed it to gain a little more velocity, then settled into an ancient rhythm, a rhythm that would remain unchanged for the next seven-hundred twenty-six miles. It was late August; the skies erupted with dense and boisterous clouds.

With flight speeds of up to sixty miles per hour and one-thousand feet above the calm sea it would be fourteen hours before the bird's keen eyes, two hundred times more powerful than a humans, spied the island of Key West in the distance. It was the first land Little Binky had seen since skirting the north coast of Cuba and crossing over the Gulf Stream.

With no thought of failure, the determined pigeon soared northwest towards her loft on Petronia Street.

~ ~ ~

The southernmost city's streets were sparsely populated at six AM as Little Binky hit the guano slicked landing board, fifteen hours after leaving the isolated rooftop in Port au Prince.

The barely winded bird strutted into the loft, beaked a couple of corn kernels, fluffed herself and took a nap.

Nearby, the owner of the loft, Miguel Santoro strutted out of a local eating place after consuming a meal of black beans, pounded pork, choked chicken and guava duff. Miguel was well aware, as were his neighbors, of his digestive failings and decided for the sake of all concerned that he would not go into or near an enclosed space after such a meal. The sixteen racing pigeons in his loft appreciated Santoro's courtesy and cooed politely.

It was later that day before Santoro ventured into the loft and noticed a message pod on Little Binky's leg. He also noted that Mahvalis, one of his favorites, had not returned to the loft.

Well, Santoro thought sadly, it's not unusual in the long distance flying routes, lots of predators up in the sky. He removed the message pod and gently patted Little Binky on the butt feathers. Returning to his cigar maker's cottage, he opened a bottle of *Barbancourt* rum, took a hefty slug, then sat down with a sigh and opened the tube. Slowly, a piece of fragile blue paper slipped out onto the table.

~ ~ ~

Smith, the RSO left the hotel after comparing a few notes with Rene Crevecoeur and went back to his office at the Embassy. There he took off his jacket and tie, took a bottle of Scotch out of his desk drawer and poured himself a stiff one. He was the only person at the Embassy except the Marine guard, so protocol was no longer necessary. Truth be told, since he wasn't a Foreign Service Officer he didn't get many visits from the rest of the staff. The only person at the Embassy who knew Smith's actual assignment was the Ambassador, who stayed away from him. Considering the difference in their status, most interpreted the distance as distain. It wasn't – it was fear. Either way, Smith wanted distance, and he got it.

What to make of the events at the hotel? A U.S. military member shot and killed by a female shooter. He didn't want to use the word "assassin" until the facts warranted it. Silenced .22 weapons weren't the local style. The Haitian criminal class went in for large caliber and bad marksmanship. The high body count at Haitian crime scenes tended to reflect incompetence as much as blood lust. This lady was certainly not incompetent, so she was likely not a common criminal, perhaps not even Haitian. There were two military personnel at the table. No one, inside of a mile, could have confused the two. The black kid was killed for a reason. The only thing that bystanders could have known about him was that he was from Key West and knew the town and the local notables well. Considering the summary of the conversation between then Slav and the Cuban, Key West was the only common denominator.

What made Key West so important?

Also, Da Turtle's name had come up again. Smith was having, Da Turtle followed and Da Turtle, in Smith's opinion, was being seen entirely too often with Rene

25

Crevecoeur. At first Smith had been inclined to think that this familiarity was a simple case of graft, Da Turtle appeared to have money and Crevecoeur, predictably, wanted a cut. Nothing sinister there. Smith had his vices and was willing to give Crevecoeur room for his. Now he wasn't so sure. Crevecoeur may be getting sloppy, or greedy, or running his own operation for his own purposes, or a combination of the three. On the to-do list, discreetly finding out what was going on with young Renee, and Da Turtle.

The next thing on the list...pigeons.

Smith was getting heartily sick of pigeons. What were they involved in here in Haiti? Lots of talk about International Pigeon Racing, but Haiti wasn't on the circuit and there were maybe two people in the country who could afford it. File all the above under possible, but unlikely and keep looking

Considering he had been hectoring his counterparts at NSA about signals coming from the mysterious valley and they had detected the square root of zero, this might mean something. Unsophisticated didn't mean stupid. Frequently it meant the contrary, as Smith had learned during Operation Phoenix many years ago. Read up on courier pigeons. Or, pigeon couriers.

The valley? The valley that Smith and Crevecoeur had discussed was a nearly empty depression located in the center of Haiti. There was a road, or so the map indicated, although Smith knew from personal observation that it wasn't even a first-rate goat track. Normally a few peasants, goats and banana trees, but nothing of interest. Suddenly, a decision by someone senior in the government advised this valley was forbidden to all but a select few. It was such a matter of how few, that even Crevecoeur wasn't allowed in. Just as interesting was that no one could track down who made the decision. Smith had sent a local contact in. Twice. The first time the contact reported white men in the area. The second time Smith's man didn't make it back. No word.

Now, for loose ends. The Slav, the Cuban and the

Polynesian girl, his sources would find them if they were still in Haiti and Smith could find out if and when they had left. If the Slav and Cuban weren't U.S. citizens, charge them with something and have the locals beat the hell out of them. Most likely Smith would learn something, even if that something was their pain threshold. Something for the file. The girl was almost certainly a French national. Was she also the shooter? Smith would have to have lunch with his French counterpart.

Smith finished the drink, "One a Day" was his motto. Smith was a man of great self-discipline. He also had an almost unique talent in his Service. He had an orderly mind that thrived on disorder. Trained as a mathematician, he was originally recruited for his ability to discern patterns in data streams. He was one of the first to recognize that Da ta didn't support the notion the U.S. had cut the flow of arms to the Mekong Delta, hence his time with Operation Phoenix. The fact that Smith was right didn't endear him to his boss. His "interview technique" as it was politely put, didn't endear him to the new intelligence leadership either, so he was stuck in staff assignments in Washington. "Brilliant but often off the Reservation" was a comment in one of his fitness reports.

Washington assignments did offer one unexpected benefit. When his wife started what was eventually to become a futile series of cancer treatments, Smith became familiar with Johns Hopkins hospital and University. After his wife's death, he eventually earned his MA and PhD in Behavioral Psychology. When he went back in the field he soon developed a reputation as the Service's own version of "Hannibal Lecter" for his ability to turn anyone's strengths and weaknesses against them ("reading and editing" was Smith's term). He became greatly respected, and feared. He was a hard man for hard situations. Now that he was older his cover was often as an old fool that being fobbed off on someone prior to eventual retirement. Think Haiti.

The next afternoon Smith had lunch with his French counterpart at the Café International.

27

They were being served, as luck would have it, by an obnoxious waiter who was also one of Smith's unwitting sources. About halfway through the meal, the waiter told Smith that Smith had an urgent phone call. There were too few working phones in the country for this to be a coincidence, Smith thought. Someone wanted to ruin his lunch. Still, a joke was a joke, he'd look for the punchline. As Smith headed for the certainly-non-operational phone, he was accosted by the Chef.

"Mister Smith, how is your luncheon? I ask this because your elevated tastes have endeared you to the staff."

"I thought it was because I pay in a currency that someone has actually heard of."

"That too. It is precisely because of that I bring you this little gift. For a small fee, of course. "

"Of course. How could I think otherwise?" A small gift for your grandchildren?

"Small fee was a figure of speech." "Do you have something larger than a fiver"?

"Oh, I meant fifty five. Alright, one hundred fifty five. How my mind wanders."

"Indeed. I found this little bauble in the street. It seems to have fallen from the roof."

"What, exactly, is on the roof?" I asked.

"A pigeon coop for, I think the English term is, carrier pigeons. *Le Tortu* is very fond of their services."

"As am I. Thank you Paul."

Never doubt the efficacy of prayer thought Smith, as he walked back to the table. When he got back to the office, he put on a mask and set of surgical gloves, opened the small container and pulled out a tightly wrapped sheet of onion paper. In the back of his mind he thought to himself, "I only know of one person in the world who could actually find this type of paper. Christ – he lives in Key West." Then he looked at the sheet of onion skin paper. The message was "You are dead!" Just then, his intercom came on. The Marine guard at Post One was on the line. "Commissioner Crevecoeur to see you sir."

The Polynesian woman caught everyone's attention as she entered Café International. After all, her dress was very tight, clinging to her curves like Saran-Wrap. She often used her looks to her advantage, distracting men as she extracted information. Moana Jones was a reporter, an international correspondent, and appeared to be onto a big story. A source had confirmed that Da Turtle was planning to fix the FCI World Championship pigeon races. The 36th Olympiad was coming up in in Brussels. Millions of dollars were at stake.

Moana smiled as she recalled Da Turtle's business card. "I fix things," it said. How was that for truth in advertising?

Word had it he was working for a Slavic man, the minion of a wealthy Englishman who was betting heavily on the outcome of the upcoming World Championship. The Slav had been dispatched to oversee the transaction, for Da Turtle had a reputation of being slippery.

Last year, (according to incautious gossip,) Da Turtle had fixed the America's Cup Races, but the winning yacht turned out to be one he'd backed, not the team he'd been hired to make win the championship trophy. But who could complain about failure to deliver when the activity had been illegal in the first place.

That Da Turtle was a sly one, no one had any doubt and if he could fix a yacht race, why not a pigeon race?

Just then, Moana spotted the man she was looking for, a character named Smith. He was sitting at a table with the police commandant, Rene Crevecoeur. She knew Smith worked at the Embassy, but she suspected his duties went well beyond a liaison with the Haitian government. It was said even the *Ton-Ton* feared him. If anyone knew where to find the elusive Turtle, he would.

"Monsieur Smith, I apologize for interrupting your lunch," Moana said. She nodded at Crevecoeur as she approached the table. "but I hoped I could I have a minute of your time?" She flashed him and Rene Crevecoeur a dazzling smile, one that could cause the meltdown of a nuclear reactor.

"Say, are you Polynesian?" Smith blurted when he looked up.

"By birth," she replied. "But before you get carried away with your South Sea fantasies, I must tell you that I am a married woman."

"Married?"

"Yes, as of last night. I was swept off my feet by an American sailor and we tied the knot. Impulsive perhaps, but I've always had a thing for big redheads."

"Oh, well, congratulations," Smith mumbled. It seemed like he was always a day late when it came to attractive women. Not that there would be any point in pursuing this one.

She presented him with her International Herald Tribune press credentials. "I am working on an important story. I hope you can help me find an American lawyer who is known as Da Turtle. I don't know his real name."

"As a matter of fact, I have this person of interest under surveillance at this very moment. He's held a number of recent meetings with my friend here, Police Commandant Crevecoeur. I was hoping he might shed some light on what this mysterious little man is up to. He's on the Embassy's watch list."

Rene Crevecoeur held up his hands in protest.

"I know nothing of this American lawyer, other than a few stray facts. Jimmy Da Turtle is based in Key West, was trained in a Jesuit monastery before entering the practice of law. He is said to be a master debater. His law degree was acquired by mail order, I'm told. He safely uses Key West as his base for international intrigue because the sly rascal holds incriminating evidence against the entire city government of that small island. Photographs of them in compromising circumstances, caught in the VIP Lounge of Louie Rock's Pimps 'n Ho's Ball during several past Fantasy Fest events. That's the way he operates, by subornation, blackmail, and bribes."

"Why have you been meeting with him?" pressured Smith for this new information.

"He wants me to introduce him Monsieur Jean Lavec, the Minister of Agriculture. Some business deal he has in mind. Perhaps I gave him the idea I was close friends with Lavec and could arrange such a meeting."

Moana asked, "What does Minister Lavec have to do with *palomas* ... pigeons, I mean?"

"Pigeons? I have no idea," said Crevecoeur.

"Don't talk to me about pigeons," scowled Smith. "They are carriers of death."

"Death? Surely you jest."

"No, that is what I was about to tell you when this beautiful woman walked up. I received a death threat delivered by a courier pigeon."

"A death threat!" shouted Rene Crevecoeur, leaping from the table.

"Quiet, please," shushed Smith. "You will upset the other patrons."

"You should get a gun, Monsieur Smith," suggested the woman. "Just to be safe."

"This may be the last time I'll have lunch with you for awhile, Smith," Crevecoeur said, "You're a Turtle target now."

"Gentlemen," interrupted Moana Jones. "I urgently need to speak with this vile Turtle man. I have a deadline. Can you tell me where I might find him?"

"You're going nowhere," said Rene Crevecoeur, slapping handcuffs around her wrist. "You are under arrest for the murder of Levon J. Perry."

Lavon Perry awoke with a jolt, his stiffened limbs twitching like a marionette. The fragments of ghoulish nightmares flooding his subconscious began to recede. Images of strange animal forms lurking in dark recesses gave way to the vision of an exotic dark-skinned woman leaning over him, chanting in an unfamiliar tongue.

As Marie Lavoisier saw the light of cognition begin to flicker in Lavon's eyes, she shook her *asson* vigorously over his heart, hastening his return to the world of the living. Although this had been her first summoning of a *baka*,

Marie concluded the reanimation ritual with the calm assurance of an accomplished practitioner. Passing a soothing hand over Lavon's still-cold forehead, she gently guided him back from the spirit realm.

The lovely apparition that filled Lavon's eyes on first awakening was suddenly displaced by a much less appealing sight: the large head of a Da Turtle. Not a marine amphibian, but the Key West lawyer known by that moniker. The disconcerting sight of the Mephistophelian Turtle staring at him triggered dim memories of the moments preceding his voyage to the netherworld. Lavon recalled drinking at the Karibe's outdoor bar with Boats, and sighting Da Turtle; but the elusive lawyer slipped away before a proper introduction could be made, and then.....a sharp pain in the forehead, lights out. Other figures began to emerge in his slowly opening mind's eye: a black-clad English dude distractedly chewing on a straw; the nattily-attired waiter bringing one too many drinks; and passing quietly along the perimeter of the bar, the lovely Polynesian reporter whose trail they had followed to the Karibe. But those images vanished as quickly as they appeared, a predictable consequence of having a bullet lodged in one's frontal lobe.

With the delicate neural pathways of his memory blocked by a lead slug, Lavon wasn't able to provide much in the way of answers to the lawyer's probing questions. Displaying no hint of frustration over his inability to extract information via his formidable inquisitorial skills, Da Turtle pressed some American currency into Marie's hand and set out for Rene Crevecoeur's office. Having encouraged the Police Commandant , by delivery of the customary emolument, to charge that bothersome reporter with Lavon's murder, Da Turtle now felt obligated to inform Crevecoeur that an essential element of that criminal charge, i.e. a corpse, was now absent. This was obviously a fatal flaw in a murder prosecution, even within the notoriously corrupt justice system overseen by the *Cour de Cassation.*

Da Turtle wasn't pleased by Moana's release from custody. He would have preferred that she remain confined, incommunicado, in a Port au Prince jail, where her considerable charm would avail her nothing in the way of information about his nefarious schemes. He had managed to mislead her by spreading a "Cuban rumor" of an elaborate plot to fix the forthcoming World Championship of pigeon-racing, a neat piece of disinformation that seemed credible given his renown as a fixer. Now she'd soon be back on his trail. And back home, Det. Lt. Cass would be expecting an answer to the question, who shot his Godson, Lavon?

Da Turtle viewed conflict of interest not as an ethical issue, but as an opportunity. Playing both sides of a game doubled potential profit, and more importantly, averted the boredom and predictability of complying with conventional legal mores. Da Turtle 's flexible approach to client loyalty enabled him to collect retainer payments from a police-protected smuggling ring based in Key West, while simultaneously serving as consigliere to the ring's competitors throughout the Caribbean. Now he found himself engaged in a high-stakes game of cat & mouse...and pigeons.

The idea of using pigeons as inter-island couriers to evade law enforcement snooping didn't originate with Da Turtle, but he had perfected it. Coupled with creative misuse of attorney-client privilege, his pigeon network had proved to be an effective and highly profitable means of evading DEA's ever-listening ear. And the information contained in those pigeon-borne capsules sometimes proved to be of value not only to the intended recipients, but also to competitors willing to pay Da Turtle a handsome "finder's fee" for sharing it. To avoid detection of his duplicity, the devious lawyer resorted to simple but ingenious ruses, most recently engineering a pigeon heist in Haiti ... and then arranging to be retained to investigate it.

Upon arriving at Rene Crevecoeur's office, Da Turtle exchanged his unwelcome news with the Police

Commandant. Crevecoeur was disgruntled to learn that the high-profile murder case on which he had planned to coast into retirement was going nowhere. Da Turtle was equally unhappy to hear that a pigeon-borne capsule had found its way into the hands of RSO Smith. The heat was spiking in Haiti; a strategic retreat appeared to be in order.

The two engaged in desultory conversation for about a quarter of an hour before Da Turtle rose and stated, "Keep me informed Rene," then let himself out by the Commandant's private passage which terminated in the quiet street behind Police Headquarters.

Rene sat pensively behind his rather large and tastefully appointed desk. The silence of the room was only interrupted by the rhythmic tapping of his pen upon the palm of his left hand. This action in conjunction with the slow nodding of his head was Rene Crevecoeur's outward display of satisfaction.

Yes, the tableau it marches nicely, Rene mused to himself as he rose from his chair and crossed the long room. Looking out the window he observed the retreating figure of Da Turtle and thought to himself, he now promenades to consult with his confidant Email at the Bistro International, alas the perfect venue for the cast of suitably costumed actors, carefully posed by Da Turtle.

A soft buzzing caught Rene's attention and he deftly moved across the room and carefully lifted the phone receiver. "Yes," he spoke into the instrument.

A soft female voice replied, "RSO Smith to speak with the Commandant."

"Put him through," was Rene's reply. "Monsieur Smith, Commandant Crevecoeur, how may I be of service?"

"You can start by giving me an explanation for this cause of death in the Levon Perry case." Suicide, now really Rene, suicide, have you all taken leave of your senses?"" How can I possibly forward this report to Washington," Smith groaned. "Just because you do not like the verdict does not make it untrue," Rene replied in his most avuncular manner. "Don't play paw-paw Rene with me, I know you have something on with that Key West lawyer Da Turtle," replied the RSO. "You know Rene, so far you and I have enjoyed a good working relationship, let's try not to spoil it," implored Smith. "But of course," the Commandant replied. "This unpleasantness will soon pass and all will be fine, Au Revoir."

Rene smiled as he placed the receiver back upon the phone. Poor RSO Smith, I do truly dislike deceiving him so, Rene thought out loud, but it must be done. Of course the police verdict of suicide was a complete farce, but no worse than that diaphanous comedy plot about pigeons, floated by the mischievous Turtle.

Rene shrugged his shoulders, gently rubbed his chin and commented quietly to himself, "One must use a petard to impel people and events into motion, without the motion there can be no information and without the information, we are nowhere in this game."

Yes, nowhere was the exact position at this moment in matters pertaining to the affairs of Da Turtle . The Commandant knew from experience that where you find Da Turtle one also finds money and *argent*, was something Rene Crevecoeur was particularly fond of. His agent in the south of France informed him of a villa at Cap Ferrat that had recently come on the market and could be had for a knocked-down price. Time was of the essence, although he could make the purchase, it would leave Rene with little working capital, and he did so wish to retire in style.

Fortune had grinned and sent Da Turtle in his direction, Rene contemplated, now I must make the most of this good piece of luck. But how? Every aspect of the game remains so dark, it is so frustrating, he mused.

Placing Moana back on the street was his hope of setting events in motion. Who was she? No record of her came back from his inquiries through the usual channels. The only thing he did know was that she was not a journalist. Far too many split infinitives in her brief statement, no, more the chanteuse than the reporter in that one. But, still she did have some manner of effect on Da

35

Turtle .

The Commandant had just settled back in his chair to follow this line of contemplation when the phone buzzed. He lifted the receiver and was about to speak when an excited voice announced, "Gun shots have been reported at the Café International , Da Turtle may be down!"

~ ~ ~

Despite the ambient brilliance of his mind, it had never occurred to Da Turtle that one day he might be the prey, not the predator. In his attempt to put two and two together in this particular scheme, he came up one digit short and uncomfortably realized that he might be the bull's-eye in this target of international intrigue.

He glanced around the sparsely populated café and waited for his *café avec une boulette de viande* to arrive. He looked down and noticed a slight tremor in his unusually small, claw-like hands, hands accustomed to holding only a pen, a penis, or a pussy. He knew that in two cases the tremors might not affect or might even enhance his performance, but the idea of ruining a fine nib because of some spasmodic sense of guilt overwhelmed him and he realized, perhaps for the first time, that his balancing act, his power plays between adversaries may have created more enemies than friends.

"Would anyone really try to ki ..."

Da Turtle's query was left unfinished as his keen eyes caught a muzzle flash in the far corner of the room near the ladies *toilette.* Thankfully, his reptilian instincts allowed him to instantly tuck his head down between his shoulders and dive to the floor in a turtlish ball. Belying his moniker, Da Turtle scuttled rapidly across the unwashed terrazzo floor on all fours, out the back door and into another stench ridden-alley.

Exiting, if you can crawling across the floor on your belly exiting, the *Allee de Puanteure,* behind the Café, Da Turtle 's mind over- revved like a fine tuned weed-whacker. The gunshot, the attendant whizzing sound and impact in the wall above his head had accelerated his thinking and he uneasily grasped the idea that the bullet hole in Lavon's re-animated head was not supposed to be there. It had been meant for him. Mortality flooded over Da Turtle like a clogged toilet and although he had faithfully ascribed to the attributes of the long-lived terrapin, he recognized his time on this orbiting dirt ball called Earth might not be as lengthy as he would prefer

~ ~ ~

It was no wonder Moana Jones was upset, it was the second time she tried to whack Da Turtle and missed. She still felt bad about nailing the unwitting Coast Guard guy and was thankful that this time it appeared her misspent bullet had only penetrated the wall of the men's room. Moana couldn't know that the hollow-point bullet blew the condom dispenser off the bathroom wall, but she would've been pleased.

Exiting the *Café International,* she heard the familiar sound of sirens but showed little concern as she pushed open the front doors and slipped out disguised as a humble service worker. Although she was, or least had been, employed by the *International Herald Tribune,* her desire for money, men and mayhem was not satisfied by the dreary job of reporting on other people's dreary lives. She needed and had a side job.

Moana wanted a life of her own and at the same time hoped that no one would report on hers as she had on theirs. She'd taken an "Erasure" contract on Da Turtle from an unknown source in the Bahamas who delivered a generous deposit to her account in Grand Cayman. There was no explanation for the ordered erasure only the words, "Find Da Turtle-Kill Da Turtle-he make big mess-Send shell for souvenir to hang on shit house wall."

~ ~ ~

Several miles away from the *Cafe,* far above the stench and over-copulated population of *Port au Prince,* a thin British expatriate stood with hands gripping the balcony railing of his small, but elegant hillside home. The man looked a great deal like the waiter in the *KARIBE* on the night of Lavon's temporary demise. He glanced down towards the city below and glimpsed what he called, "An unacceptable blend of man and nature." He lit a fat Cuban cigar.

For many years, the thin man had reflected on the ambiguity of the universe and rather quickly came to realize that no one was in charge. He therefore felt free to play any game he chose.

The narrow fellow paused and expelled what he affectionately called, *"Le vent de la nuit,* the wind of the night. Nor was he was a soulless man, it was simply that he realized the limited amount of soul available in his case and decided to employ it only when necessary. In this instance, there was no need for soul. The fact that the man, known as Da Turtle, the subject of many nasty songs and bumper stickers, was wreaking havoc throughout the Caribbean and had finally become entangled in his own web was reason enough.

The thin man wished he could be there to witness Da Turtle's demise, but his tailor at Limpool's of London had rung him up this morning and advised his SPF 30 jodhpurs and breathable Kevlar, albino mole-hair undergarments were complete and awaiting final fitting and strategic monogram application.

Fortunately, the thin man was wealthy for he had spent a fortune on monograms. Once, forced to wear un-monogrammed clothing, he steadfastly refused and instead stood naked through his entire Episcopalian confirmation ceremony. To this day his underwear was monogrammed on both sides of the waistband, a precaution should anyone attempt to steal them and wear them inside out. The thin man's mind never stopped working, nor did it ever accomplish much. But today, today was different, today Da Turtle would withdraw into his unfurnished shell for the last time.

The thin man turned at the sound of his monkey-skull doorbell. He opened the heavy wooden entry to find a man dressed all in black standing at his doorstep, hundreds of unreadable bookmarks drooped from his bulging pockets.

"Lord Pimlico Gorton Blackstraw! What a pleasure!" the narrow man said with a thin-lipped smile.

"Ah, DMD! The pleasure is mine."

"What brings you up the hill, tired of the lowland *chatte*?" the thin man, known only by his monogram initials, inquired.

"I've run out of bloody cocktail straws...Just kidding. I have, unfortunately, been unable to locate Da Turtle again."

"This 'Da Turtle' fellow seems to thrown a bit of turd on the patch, but I have solved the problem," DMD said, "my friend and I will no longer require your services. I want to thank you for all you've done." The thin man reached down and pulled a small box out of his smoking jacket.

"I had these custom-made for you in Switzerland," DMD said with a more than generous smile.

"That's not necessary, but veddy kind," Blackstraw replied.

"Here, let me show you," DMD said. He reached into the box and withdrew one of several sparkling, monogrammed black cocktail straws.

"Beautiful," Lord Blackstraw commented, noticing the letters DMD stenciled on the remaining straw shafts.

DMD held the straw even closer to Blackstraw' s face and then without warning, reached to the side and drove the straw deep into Blackstraw' s right ear.

DMD drew back, expecting a violent reaction and a nauseating and perhaps dreadful display of unexpected death. Instead, Lord Pimlico Blackstraw did not seem to notice. He simply smiled, plucked the small gift box from the thin man's hand and tucked it down the front of his pants amongst the bookmarks.

"Nice try, old bean, many thanks and good luck...with Life." Blackstraw nodded towards the thin man, headed for the door and continued in a sing-song voice,

"Gotta go on down to Zombie town, where death is overrated.

*I'm sure I'll see you there, once **your** soul has been*

deflated."

The thin man was not pleased with the results of his attempted homicide.

"What the fuck, doesn't anyone die and stay dead around here anymore?"

Miguel Santoro felt sick. Real sick. The Turtle was too experienced in such matters to have a message in his handwriting and covered with his DNA in circulation. He had trained his minions to copy each message, then burn the original Even a dim-wit like Santoro could get that part right, or so the Turtle had thought. Santoro had opened the pigeon's message capsule and read the message. Then he copied it and burned the original. A man of limited education, he didn't read English well, so it took him a while to copy, then decipher the message. The original had read "Be in the right place or you are dead." Santoro's transcription read "Be in the right plague or you are dead." He saw a word he didn't recognize, "plague," and a phrase he did, "you're dead." He went to a neighbor's house to borrow a dictionary. By the time he borrowed the biggest book he had ever seen he didn't feel at all well. Then he looked up "plague." He fainted.

A few hours later, Santoro woke up and went to the hospital. It took him three hours to be admitted. The ER doctors at Lower Florida Key Hospital ("flakies" in local parlance, an appropriate term if there ever was one) were watching their favorite show, General Hospital, and waited until the conclusion. Then they discussed whether or not Nurse Dora really, really, resembled one of the more attractive female characters, and whether she was actually angling to marry a doctor. Then they had to decide which one of them she was angling for, or not. The vote was tied, so the ER was in the throes of arcane parliamentary procedure when the admitting nurse told them that one of the people in the waiting room had collapsed. They stopped pretending to be doctors on TV and started to pretend to be doctors in real life. No one was fooled.

Santoro didn't help himself by emitting the foulest

stench to be smelled in Christendom in at least five hundred years. The ER staff donned oxygen masks, placed Santoro under the largest exhaust vent they could find, then fell back through sealed doors to regroup.

"Should we warn anyone downwind?" asked a newly minted resident.

"No," said the senior doctor. "It should be pretty well dissipated by the time it gets to Key Haven. In any case, with all the jet fuel smell, who would know? Don't panic the public is what I say."

The rest of the staff agreed. They all knew about Santoro and his digestive challenges. The fact that they had reached a decision stiffened all spines, so, after checking their oxygen supply they sallied forth, back to where they had left Santoro. He wasn't there. After an hour's frantic search, they scratched Santoro's name from the admissions log and hoped for the best.

A naked-from-the-waist-down Santoro was located by the Key West police, running as fast and as far as a man as obese as Santoro could run across the Cow Key Channel bridge. Santoro told the booking sergeant that he was being poisoned by a Da Turtle, or a pigeon, or a dictionary, the sergeant couldn't really tell. Either way, the jail staff placed a large exhaust fan in a cell and put Santoro in the cell with it.

He stayed until his son bailed him out the next day. Santoro left the jail with all of the car's windows down and a blind fear of Da Turtle, pigeons, and dictionaries. He washed his hands of the whole affair. Never again would he do a favor for Da Turtle. It wasn't funny. As luck would have it, he never sent a return message that he had not gone to "the right place" – Key West Police Headquarters.

~ ~ ~

The week didn't start well when the quarterdeck watch called me, "Sir, (I was starting to prefer *Gran Rouge*, odd,) your wife is on the line. Please let me transfer her call."

"You must be mistaken. I'm not married. "

"Sir, that's what I told her, but she is pretty adamant

about it. Do want me to put the call through? Are congratulations in order?"

This was bad even for a Monday.

"Not yet, but O.K., go ahead. I'll take the call."

"It's me, Moana, and I am in real trouble. I'm still in Haiti. I was arrested, then released for no reason I can think of. I need money for lawyers and bribe money for Commandant Crevecoeur, and I need it now."

"You a big fan of 1950's American TV ?"

"No, why on earth for?"

"Because if you were, the phrase "Lucy, you got some 'splaining to do" would ring a bell. What in hell are you talking about and why are you telling people that we are married? And as long as I'm asking questions, what were you arrested for?"

"A-I needed to get some credibility with your embassy and it seemed like a good story. B-For murder."

"O.K., A I can forgive, sort of. What about murder?"

"I didn't mean to shoot the man I shot, so it's really a case of mistaken identity.

These people are taking this too seriously. They should take a deep breath. Look at the big picture."

"Who are, 'these people'?"

"Commandant Crevecoeur and your man Smith. The judge seemed to like me, but they don't."

"Who was the man you shot." I answered my own question before she did – there was just one man shot that night, Lavon.

"The young black man you were talking to. Did you know him?"

"Yes, he was a friend of mine."

"I'm sorry. I didn't mean to. It was an accident. I was aiming at that vile creature, Da Turtle, but just as I was pulling the trigger, an odd looking waiter came running out of the kitchen with a pot of very hot tea and spilled it on me. I flinched. It happens."

"What do you mean 'it happens,' How often do you shoot people? And why do you want to kill Da Turtle?

"As often as needed, and because I promised. You are being so bourgeois. Spare me the sermon." The line went dead.

I did some quick thinking. I had three weeks leave on the books and just sold some stock. I had ability, motive and means as they used to say on cop shows.

Now I just needed permission and transportation. I called the X.O. and asked him if he had any plans. Barring an emergency, he said he didn't. We were in a maintenance period so the ship wasn't going anywhere .

~ ~ ~

Things were going better for Smith in Port au Prince. He had been staring at the

NSA decrypts of the transmissions from the mystery valley in Haiti. The NSA told him they couldn't break the code because there was no code. It was gibberish.

The only symbols were a single capital letter and a lower-case letter followed by a two-digit number, repeated in random sequences. Monkeys with a typewriter as far as they were concerned. Smith remembered the old, analog days.

Simplicity was good. Sophisticated observers often mistook the obvious for the mysterious and ignored it. Then it hit him. A capitol letter, followed by a lower case letter and a two-digit number. He was humming a Tom Lehr song when it suddenly it came to him. It was damn periodic tables! Only intellectuals could be that blind. He looked-up the periodic tables, and it became painfully obvious. There were three elements, all classified as "rare earths." Some research and a large Scotch later, he had his answer. "Rare earths" were more valuable than platinum. They were critical to the manufacture and development of sophisticated digital circuits. No rare earths, no HP calculators, no Cray supercomputer. That was just the start. There was considerable technical literature about the coming revolution in "smart devices" and how these elements would be even more critical in thirty years. The U.S., Russia, China and the Europeans were scouring the world for this stuff and he had found the guys who had found the mother lode. It was in Haiti, and someone wanted that to stay their little secret. But who and why? Not some flash frozen hippie in Key West.

For all those clowns knew, Rare Earth was a 60's rock group. No, these were some very sophisticated folks he was dealing with.

~ ~ ~

Smith was still congratulating himself for discovering the secret of the valley and the real nature of the Turtle's scheme when he got a call from a newly made friend in the Haitian National Telephone company.

"Mr. Smith, there was a call recently placed to Key West from a hotel in Cap Haitian. The caller was a woman. I thought you would like to know."

Lavon Perry staggered through the streets of Port-au-Prince, unmindful of the stench of garbage and raw sewage. The street sounds of ancient automobiles surrounded him. The chatter of bare-chested Haitians roasting corn over a steel-drum fire went unnoticed. Scrawny dogs sniffed at him as he passed.

He had a powerful headache, the worst migraine ever, as if a monkey were pounding his temples with a ball-peen hammer. He had little recognition of where he was, merely the impulse to "get back to the ship."

Being a good Coast Guardsman, Lavon knew he needed to report in because if he was found to be AWOL, he might lose shore privileges. That wouldn't do. He wanted to go bar-crawling with his friend -uh, what was his name? Big Red, wasn't that it? It was so hard to remember...

Two days had passed since Marie Lavoisier reanimated Lavon Perry and he had been wandering about the town in a daze, his thoughts completely jumbled. A bullet to the brain will do that.

Was that what had happened to him? Yes, he had been shot. But miraculously he had survived. It wasn't clear how.

Memories flooded his mind, one of a young Haitian woman leaning over him, flanked by the wizened face of a white man. He couldn't put a name to either of these visages, but the man reminded him vaguely of ... a Da Turtle?

He knew he had to clean himself up before reporting back to his ship. He spotted a ramshackle bar with a hand-painted sign proclaiming it to be Waldo's Watering Hole. He hobbled inside, heading toward the bathroom.

"Hey!" shouted the mahogany-skinned man behind the bar. But on taking a closer look, the bartender clammed up, made the sign of the cross, and hurried out the side door. "*Zombie*," he muttered – the Creole word that denotes the living dead.

Harvard ethnobotanist Wade Davis postulated that zombies were not really dead, merely people who had been put into a death-like state by a combination of puffer fish venom and toad venom (with a dollop of a hallucinogen called tetrodotoxin).

But Lavon was an argument to the contrary. He had a bullet hole in the center of his forehead, like a third eye.

He examined his countenance in the grimy bathroom mirror. The funeral home had touched up the wound using brown facial putty. You could hardly see it against his dark skin. But his clothing was wrinkled and streaked with mud, a result of the rough handling of his body before it got to Marie Lavoisier. Morgue attendants have little concern for their lifeless charges.

Lavon brushed off the dirt best he could, his arm motions jerky and uncoordinated. He'd probably receive demerits for his shabby appearance. The Coast Guard had rigorous standards.

Dimly, Lavon knew he had to find Big Red. His friend would help him get back on the ship, tidy him up, take him to sickbay.

He didn't feel well.

What was the story with that Turtle guy, anyway? Hadn't he seen the weird little man before? Maybe right before he was shot.

Lavon examined the wound in the bathroom mirror.

Luckily, it had only been a flesh wound. Otherwise, a bullet to the head could kill you, right?

A new memory came drifting by, like a leaf on a stream. Another face: a beautiful Eurasian woman. Or was she Polynesian? That newspaper reporter that Big Red had been smitten with. What about her?

At the edge of his memory floated still another image, the Polynesian woman with a gun in her hand. Had she shot him? Or was she trying to shoot Da Turtle ? It was all very confusing.

He heard sirens. Had the bartender called the shore patrol? Better them than the Ton-Ton Macoute. Those black-suited boys would chop you up with a machete. No coming back from that.

His first inclination was to wait for the shore patrol. They would take him to Big Red. He needed to reach his friend.

At the last minute he panicked, racing out the side door of Waldo's Watering Hole, into a narrow alley, stumbling around a crumbling brick corner, and rushing into the searing sunlight of a wide, bustling boulevard.

Up ahead he could see the façade of an elegant restaurant. *Ajan Soulye*, the marquee said. That meant Silver Slipper. For some reason he seemed pulled toward the restaurant as if in the grip of an alien tractor beam.

At the door of the Silver Slipper, he hesitated. Did he dare risk causing alarm as he had at the bar? He debated going inside.

While he hesitated, the restaurant's double doors swung open and out stepped a large man with a red beard, a beautiful woman on his arm. The man was nattily dressed in a pressed white Coast Guard uniform; the woman wore a slinky dress that emphasized her ample breasts and curvy hips. It was Big Red and the Polynesian woman!

"A-y-g-b-y," Lavon grunted, unable to get out a greeting.

The woman, Moana, that was her name, reached into her purse and extracted a pistol. She pointed it at Lavon

46

and – *ka-bam!* – shot him in the right eye. He dropped like a rock.

"W-why did you do that?" her oversized companion sputtered. "That was my friend Lavon."

"It was his fault that I missed Da Turtle. He screwed up everything. If I could, I'd kill him *three* times."

"But my dear ..."

"Shut up, you fool. I may as well kill you too. You've proven useless in getting me any closer to that vile little Da Turtle." She pointed the gun directly at Big Red's flushed red face. Her finger tightened on the trigger. "I may enjoy being a widow," she smirked. "Will I inherit anything?"

"Wait!" shouted a voice behind her.

Extending an upraised hand to reinforce his verbal command, Rene Crevecoeur stepped forward authoritatively, placing himself squarely between Moana and Big Red. Fixing his gaze on Moana's twin dark orbs rather than the pistol in her hand or her formidable physique, Rene announced in a sonorous baritone, "One more dead body and you will be spending the rest of a short miserable life starving and dodging rats in the national prison. "

Her luscious lips contorting into a pout, Moana sighed, "I guess I'll be going there anyway; there's a sailor laying on the floor over there with a bullet in his head."

Casting a practiced eye over Lavon's remains, the Police Commandant replied, "Here it is not murder to dispatch a Zombie to the land of the dead; but the large redheaded target in your sights is obviously among the living; Drop your weapon." Lowering her pistol, the sultry beauty shrugged her shoulders; "Sorry; guess I was just frustrated; that wiry little Zombie was all that stood between me and my prey. If it weren't for him, I'd already have collected a bounty for bagging a Da Turtle." Crevecoeur immediately caught her reference to the reptilian lawyer.

"No bounty is worth incurring the wrath of that devious creature or his cold-hearted clients," Crevecoeur replied.

As Commandant Crevecoeur relieved Moana of her

pistol, she remarked wryly, "It appears I flunked Assassination 101. Scared off the prey. By now, Da Turtle is probably on his way back to Key West, where no one can touch him." Although Crevecoeur knew otherwise, he kept that knowledge to himself.

A few days previously, the Police Commandant had arranged for the wily lawyer, who was renowned for his uncanny knack of surfacing at the center of convoluted schemes, to meet with Minister Lavec. The ostensible subject of that meeting , an "organic farming venture," seemed an unlikely enterprise for the Da Turtle's local cohorts, whose planting expertise was limited to depositing their victims' remains in unmarked graves. Rumors of fresh dig sites in the Valley had reached Crevecoeur shortly after Smith's operatives reported an uptick in coded radio transmissions from that area. Those mystery signals ceased abruptly at about the same time that Da Turtle surfaced in Port au Prince. A coincidence, unlikely in Haiti, where little could be ascribed to mere chance.

Having alertly ducked the bullet that Moana fired in his direction, Da Turtle retracted into his shell. Not the hardened carapace sheltering his namesakes in the Order Testudines, but a figurative shell of secret hiding places and passages where he could elude detection. His friend the Police Commandant had once again proven useful, arranging a meeting with the Minister of Agriculture, and assuring safe passage from the Capitol to the site of a clandestine exploratory mining operation in the remote *Savannah Mystique*. Da Turtle expressed his appreciation for Rene's courtesies in the customary manner a delivery of a generous gratuity, sufficient to enable Crevecoeur to complete his purchase of the Cap Ferrat villa to which he hoped to retire. Neither the entrepreneurial public servant nor the amoral attorney suffered the slightest pang of guilt over this mutually-beneficial arrangement, which could easily pass scrutiny in the Ethics-Free zones of Port au Prince and Key West.

The *Savannah Mystique* (mysterious valley) is a cloud-shrouded enclave occupied by descendants of the maroons , escaped slaves who in the late 18th Century had fled their captors, taking refuge in remote regions of Hispaniola. Now, more than two centuries later, the valley 's denizens remained isolated from the outside world, beyond the reach of Port au Prince officialdom. Only the most fearless pale-skinned adventurers dared venture there, and of those, a mere handful eventually returned to what passed for civilization elsewhere in Haiti. Lord Gorton Pimlico Blackstraw was one of those few, re-emerging in Port au Prince several years after he vanished into the *Savannah Mystique*. He returned a changed man.

Before embarking on a journey into the heart of darkness, his lordship typified the vacuous inebriants who comprise the voluntarily exiled British nobility, getting by in the tropics on an inherited title, a modest monthly remittance, and a daily ration of rum. The opprobrious simile, "drunk as a Lord," fit him like a well-tailored vest, and he distinguished himself in no discernible manner. He lacked even the capacity common to the non-commoner windbags who comprise the British Upper House, to engage in verbose rhetorical jousts. But when he reappeared in Port au Prince after a long absence, his peers noticed that he was ... ah ... different.

The drunken wastrel whom they had previously known now eschewed intoxicants, the sole reminder of his barfly past being an addictive oral fixation on black plastic cocktail straws, for which he was awarded the sobriquet "Lord Blackstraw." He also appeared impervious to pain, a singular ability that enabled him to garner thousands of dollars and pounds won in sucker bets placed by inebriated patrons of the port's tourist-trap saloons. What half-drunk tourist could resist betting that he could make the British blueblood flinch by shoving a cocktail straw into whatever orifice the tourist might choose? As one dazed sucker wondered aloud, after losing the entire contents of his wallet to a wager with Blackstraw, "Who is this guy? One of those comic book mutants?"

But the most remarkable departure from his Lordship's previously prodigal persona was that he now exhibited a marketable skill: an exceptional ability to ascertain the whereabouts of anyone whom he might be hired to find. It was Blackstone's apparent failure to exercise this heretofore- infallible tracking skill that earned him a straw through his ear from the thin man. How was it that Blackstraw hadn't been able to find the most unmistakable white man in an overwhelmingly black city? DMD suspected a double-cross; perhaps his lordship had gone rogue, and was now conspiring with Da Turtle!

Truth be told, DMD's suspicions were not unfounded: Lord Blackstraw *did* know Da Turtle 's precise location, having tracked his scuttle marks from the *Café International*, through the squalid alleys of Port au Prince, over the scalped hillsides surrounding the capitol, and into the *Savannah Mystique*. However, he had no desire to share that information with DMD and the avaricious overseas Chinese in whose company the thin man was increasingly seen. Blackstraw had heard the rumors of treasure lying buried under the thin soil of the *Savannah Mystique* and he doubted that some legendary pirate cache was suddenly attracting foreign interest to that remote land. Blackstraw owed a debt of gratitude to the valley folk who had taken him in, imparted their arcane knowledge and inducted him into their secret rituals. He realized that their isolated society could not withstand the modern-day equivalent of a gold-rush. But how to deflect an incursion by the horde of rapacious outsiders who would be drawn to the valley by rumors of mineral wealth?

His Lordship had concluded that only a masterful campaign of disinformation could secure the Valley against those foreign marauders. Fortunately, the master of deception had recently emerged from his shell, arriving at the Valley's clandestine mining site. Just the person to concoct and disseminate insidious rumors of plague, pestilence and zombies! Da Turtle was about to acquire a new client.

~ ~ ~

"Damn it!" RSO Smith ejaculated as he slammed the phone receiver back onto the instruments cradle. "Missed him again thanks to monsieur Crevecoeur," Smith hissed through clenched teeth. Rubbing his temples, Smith gazed at the ceiling fan of his small office and slowly shook his head. "Widdershins, the fan, this case, all widdershins!" The call he had just received informed him that his many hours of detective work, with the intent of locating and bringing in Da Turtle for questioning, had all been for naught. Rene Crevecoeur's people were a quarter of an hour ahead and had spirited the elusive attorney to a new location. Now he was back to square one with nothing to show for his efforts. "Great just great" he mused to himself, "outwitted by the local Creole flatfoot, yea this will go down just dandy up at Langley."

This was one of those days when Smith wished he had remained in the Army, "at least you knew who was on first in those days," he was wont to say. Yes, the rivers of Vietnam were looking pretty good right about now, a good crew, rapid promotion and a sense of satisfaction were the order of Da y back then, as opposed to the mares nest he found himself in now. "What do I tell Washington" he asked himself over and over, growing ever more despondent with each passing moment? Suddenly the depressed mood was broken by the buzz of the secured phone line. Ah, problem solved, he thought, Washington is now going to tell me. He picked up the receiver and spoke the words "RSO Smith" in a rather subdued voice. Upon hearing the voice on the line he sat bolt upright in his chair. "Yes, I see, yes, not a problem, 2000 hours, very good sir," he then rang off, leaned back in his chair, heaved an exhausted sigh and exclaimed "Great Caesar's Ghost!"

At the appointed hour Smith found himself ascending the discreet rear staircase of Rene Crevecoeur's official office. As he entered the room he noticed that Rene was not in uniform, but was attired in a very well-tailored linen suit, that rather suited him nicely. Also, he was not seated

51

behind his desk, but was comfortably recumbent in one of two sumptuous leather chairs. This setting left no doubt in Smith's mind that Rene Crevecoeur Commandant had now shifted roles to Rene Crevecoeur, Company Agent.

"Well I can't say that I am surprised," Smith smiled at Rene. I suppose it's the money, do they pay you well?"

"But of course, " Rene answered in his most genial tone of voice, then hardening a bit stated, "Let's get down to the business at hand."

"Indeed" Smith nodded, "Onward into the fog." Rene opened with, "As you already know Da Turtle is our main person of interest in these events. The others are secondary and will be dealt with after we have brought to light the various schemes of our friend *Monsieur Tortue*," Rene stated in a somewhat casual manner. "So why don't we bring him in for questioning," asked Smith?

"That would produce absolutely nothing my friend," was Crevecoeur's reply. " You see my good Mr. Smith, if you know what a man's doing, get in front of him, but if you want to guess what he's doing keep behind him" added Rene. At the moment we must stay behind Da Turtle, at least till we can discern his intentions."

"So what do we have so far?" questioned Smith.

"Precious little, that's the rub," answered Rene. "All we know at present is that Da Turtle is attempting to raise large sums of capital, with the intent of using the aforementioned to purchase real estate."

"What in the world is that guy up to," pondered Smith?

"That, my friend, is what our friends in Washington expect us to discover, along with the other characters and plots in connection with his scheme," responded Rene.

Smith laughed out loud," Other characters and plots indeed, where do we begin with this lot?"

"Let us begin with the two Coast Guard officers, Mr. Perry and the one known as Big Red, or Le Gran Rouge," Rene offered.

"Yes, start with Perry," Smith pleaded.

"Mr. Perry is alive and in the employ of Da Turtle and

the Red One is, how shall we say, an unpaid mourner,"
Rene stated emphatically. "So let me get this straight, Perry
is alive, so that means the shooter also works for Da Turtle
right?"

"Correct," answered Rene.

"So with all the shots fired all we really have is one dead
condom machine and a smitten coastie," chuckled Smith.
"But why the elaborate charade," Smith added?

"To influence his clients," responded Rene.

"I see," nodded Smith," where do the two guys,
Blackstraw and DMD fit into the scheme?"

Rene did not respond at once to Smith's question, but
rather looked thoughtful for a moment before stating that
perhaps the time had come to introduce the RSO to one of
his colleagues. Rene gestured with his left hand to the
empty room and opened his introduction with "Mr. Smith
let me introduce you to the head of Special Operations,
Commandant   Dominique   Michael   Duval."
The empty room was suddenly filled with a long thin
shadow, and RSO Smith now found himself confronted
with a pair of blue velvet Albert slippers embroidered with
the monogram DMD.

~ ~ ~

It was early evening in the *Vallée Mystérieuse*, the
Savannah Mystique, a deep, sucking gorge that had kept its
dark secrets hidden for centuries.

Nearby, a mountain stream, a tributary of the *Petite
Riviere de l'Artibonite* rattled toward the sea and tumbled
among the sacred waterfalls of the petulant *Saint d' Eau*.
The forever sound of water on rock smoothed the endless
cacophony of life and death struggles on the jungle floor
and the foreboding forest cries from above. The river flowed
past the sites of the original *Taino* inhabitants who left their
mark on the valley with mysterious petroglyphs. Many of
these ancient stone carvings were discovered by observant
wives whose husbands came home after fishing, with
ancient imprints on their buttocks from sitting on the cool
rocks. Each native ass carried a story of times long ago;

however, no one could read the mysterious indents or, perhaps chose not to.

Burnished river stones, covered with deadly algae, quietly applauded Sister Gaylord Badger's efforts as he climbed the moss covered steps and approached the front door of his deep forest Abbey.

Under the flag of unwitting innocence, The Sisters of the Shriveled Penance, an offshoot of, The Holy Order of the Shrivelled Penance, had cross bred with the well-known Sisters of Perpetual Indulgence, and fueled by anonymous donors, the Sisters had constructed a small temple where crude wooden pews housed devoted termites and pious ants prayed in perpetual silence on damp dirt floor.

The temple, a small adobe hut with a red Mediterranean-style roof and a crude cross made of dismembered, pink plastic flamingoes, flown in from Miami, had recently been buttressed by generous funding from a mysterious anglophile known only by his monogram initials, DMD. It is said that these initials were accidently but permanently embroidered on his left breast during a drunken fitting session. For reasons yet unknown, DMD had directed his emissary to deliver $2000.00 U.S., in cash to the Order every month for the last year. DMD's expressionless emissary promised that one day DMD himself would come amongst them and spread the joy of civilization and real toilet paper. The only caveat, according to the emissary, required the Order to display 8 X 10 glossy photographs of DMD's remarkable spiritual trans-formation. They were to be posted on the abbey wall near the suggestion box. This request was not a problem since DMD, the Sisters felt, had become a success story for the Abbey.

Sister Gaylord Badger peeked through the beaded door that depicted a vague image of Jimmy Hendrix. Inside, another dark-robed sister blew candles and dusted the altar. Brittle pieces of tile, mud and the occasional depleted pistol round dropped from the ceiling at odd intervals, while nearby, between the pews, another dark robe gathered spent .45 cartridges and hastily abandoned nipple clips, all apparently forgotten sacraments of the last service.

The alter, made of flattened beer cans hammered together, squeaked a strange harmony when dusted and wild monkey chatter filled jungle air so dense one had to sip the atmosphere, like fine cognac, to avoid drowning.

Sister Badger, a direct descendant of the Seminal Indian tribe, had just returned from gathering sacred herbs along the dense forest trail. He pushed the garish beads aside and paused to admire the before and after photos of their current philanthropic member, a shape changer, long distance devotee and reported fashion icon, the man known only as DMD.

The well preserved photographs had been provided by DMD's emissary, a small turtlish fellow. They hung crookedly, but profoundly, on the thin tin wall.

Since becoming an honorary Sister via mail, a significant transition of the man's spirit had become quite obvious. A pair of worn, blue velvet Albert slippers hung toe down on a rusty nail below the photos.

BEFORE TRANSITION

AFTER TRANSITION

It is said that early members of the Order, who chose not to hide their masculine features or facial hair, were characterized by the famed Haitian historian, *Madame Wooton Bella la' Rue,* as the embodiment of, "Genderfuck."

Sister Badger stapled the sacred herbs, known to devotees as, "God's Lettuce," upside down on an old *People* Magazine to dry and moved to pour a glass of *Ju Ju* water for herself. The sacred trek had been long and he'd run out of sacred rolling papers near the sacred garden.

After refreshment, he walked about the Abbey and gathered six homemade litter boxes. All of the Sisters loved cats; some Sisters said they glowed at night. He carefully emptied the contents of each out the back door and watched small feline tootsie-rolls tumble down the hill, pass thru the herb garden and meander towards the hungry valley below. Then, as he/she always did, Sister Badger refilled the trays with a local absorbent material the native Maroons called, *"Terres Rares."* He returned the litter trays to their original locations, yawned and stretched out on a pew to nap.

Maybe, it was the silence of the birds that awoke Sister Gaylord, or perhaps it was the sound of a giant Sikorsky heavy lift helicopter lowering a massive yellow bulldozer towards the bottom of the valley nearby that stirred him. Whatever the reason, Sister Badger could see a small figure wearing a parachute pack that looked like a turtle shell, leaning out the helicopter's side door and giving spastic hand signals, mostly the one-finger variety, to the curious natives gathered below.

The Caterpillar D6 set down hard in a cloud of mosquitoes, frightened Maroons and mashed banana trees. With much noise and scuffling the 20-ton bulldozer was remotely detached, then the Sky Crane pulled pitch, lifted upwards and dragged herself into the low lying jungle mist. As Gaylord's eyes followed the Sikorsky skyward he noticed a parachute descending thru the morning fog. Within seconds, the man known to the Order as The Emissary, plummeted to earth, landed ass-first in an ant hill, discarded his chute and climbed aboard the massive earth-eater. The steely beast coughed to life, belched acrid black smoke and began plowing an erratic swath thru the virgin jungle with the grinning little man at the controls. Then the D6 turned sharply and headed uphill, towards the abbey.

Da Turtle had arrived, could DMD be far behind?

~ ~ ~

There was one person in Key West who was particularly fascinated with the goings on, it was Lt. Tito "Cass" Cassamayor. Cassamayor was not a rocket scientist, he was a cheerfully self-declared corrupt cop. He knew in which closets all of the local power broker's skeletons were located. It was rumored that he had put several literal skeletons there himself, ensuring a certain freedom from open criticism. He wasn't a good cop in any ethical sense, but he was a very efficient one. A recently received FBI crime report indicated that the pigeon racing business in Haiti may be under the control of an unsavory person using it to cover illegal transmission of messages via bird courier and Haiti suddenly become an obsession of Cass's since his godson Levon had just been killed in Haiti. Cass knew why Lavon was in Haiti. He just didn't know what Haiti was doing in Key West. Instinctively he knew the two events were related and he intended to find out how. Then he intended to collect on what he thought of as a debt, but first he needed to make a house call, or in this case, a ship call.

~ ~ ~

The ship's inter com crackled.

"Sir, you have a visitor at the Quarterdeck. A Lt. Cassamayor from the KWPD is here to speak to you."

"Got it, please bring him aboard."

We met in my stateroom and shook hands. I asked him what prompted his visit. I knew him by reputation as the standing project for the FBI's government-corruption squad, but had never met him in person. He was about 5'9, heavy set but moved with a surprising agility. His handshake was better than firm. I guessed that he was probably someone who liked a close-quarters quarrel. I found out quickly enough. He threw a nasty right cross. It certainly moved me back a foot or two.

"You son of a bitch, you let Levon get killed! I know you're sorry. I know you can't bring him back. You know I don't give a damn. But now I feel better. We're even. Now, tell me what happened down there."

I rated the punch a 5, to tell the truth it was a relief. I had been kicking myself for not having stopped what happened in Haiti and I needed help in trying to find out exactly what had happened and why. Help was standing less than two feet away. So, I told him, in detail. He started to take notes and when Da Turtle's name came up his expression grew dark, it appeared he and Da Turtle were acquainted and in a not-too-friendly way.

"I do honest corruption. Take a few dollars, collect a few favors, sell some evidence, break a few legs. Not that you or anyone else is going to prove it. That son of a bitch, apparently referring to Da Turtle, does evil. Bred-in-the-bone evil and you and I are going to prove it. The guy with the pigeons, yes I know about Santoro and the birds. Santoro is stupid, even for a Conch. That fart-bomb is too stupid to know what he is mixed up in. His family was harmless enough, not mobbed-up or connected with Miami. I put them down as not especially innocent bystanders. So, the question is, what were they bystanding?"

I spoke up, " My guess is that the real operation is going on in Haiti. Key West is the nexus for money, information or both, a kind of strange exchange. After all, you think you can communicate reliably to or from Haiti without the locals becoming curious? What about banks? A large transfer of currency, bearer bonds or certificates of exchange from Haiti to anywhere are either going to be stolen by the locals or flagged by Treasury or INTERPOL in a pair of seconds. An inter-bank transfer from First State Bank of the Florida Keys or the Marathon branch of Bank of America doesn't really rate much scrutiny. A few bounces and suddenly it goes to Scotia Bank in the Caymans. Then it is too late. I used to think Lavon was killed by accident. Now I think he was killed because he knew too much about Key West. Now that I think about it, Da Turtle 's and the Slav's antennae started to quiver when Lavon said he grew up in Key West. Maybe they thought he would eventually start to make some uncomfortable connections. Either that or they were trying to get back at you for some reason. He did mention your name."

Cassamayor stood silently for a few moments and then said, "Da Turtle probably couldn't help himself. Took care of his internal security and got back at me when he knew I couldn't touch him. Well, I can touch him. Here I have jurisdiction, friendly judges and some muscle that doesn't ask questions and enjoys their work. Here is what we – not the Feds, not FDLE or KWPD – we, you and I and some friends of mine, are going to do. We are going to give our friend "Da Turtle" a compelling reason to come back here, not because he will want to but because his life will be ruined if he doesn't, and then we ruin him and make it hurt when we do."

"Where do I come in?"

"You are going to become an uncomfortable distraction. You are going to get the U.S. Government involved. They are going to make life in Haiti unbearable for that bastard. Beaters driving him out of cover and keeping him in the open. Turtles, especially our Turtle, don't like open areas.

I'm hoping that he will come here to hide. If not soon, then soon enough. You don't need to know what I'm going to do or how I'm going to do it. I don't need to know what or how you are going tom do, only that you'll hold up your end. Deal?"

"Deal. I'll make some arrangements. I'll tell you when I leave."

"Good."

Smith was thinking along the same lines in his embassy office. He had made his name in the Service during Operation Phoenix. In Vietnam he had developed, planned and executed (he loved unintentional puns) the decapitation of the Viet Cong political leadership in the Mekong Delta. Slowly, he identified the persons involved, determined who constituted their support systems, and then separated the target from the networks that provided cover, material support, communications and information. It was sometimes pretty gruesome work, but it drove the targets into the open where they could either be turned or eliminated. He preferred turned, but often wasn't given that luxury. It was good enough for guerrillas. Why not Turtles? There are lots of guerrillas., but only one Turtle, a smart Turtle, but still, just one Turtle.

So, he thought, where are we in this? We have the what, excavation of rare earths. We have the where, the mysterious valley. Not as mysterious as before. Thanks to a small pool of working construction equipment in Haiti, he had been able to trace the Sky Crane and the large bulldozer to a set of geographic coordinates, however unlikely those coordinates were. We still don't have the fun part of the how – how the opposition plans to get the rare earths out of this Godforsaken place, they will either have to build or invent infrastructure, challenging even for Da Turtle . We have the public who, Da Turtle but we don't have then hidden who, the substructure that supports him. Here Smith felt he was making progress. He was certain Crevecoeur and his associate were working for Da Turtle. Smith had to give the Haitians credit for moral clarity; if you can't find enough of the living, recruit the sort-of-living. He was still wondering if the man Levon, assuming he actually was or had been a man, was a zombie. The problem was, zombie or not – what were they doing for Da Turtle and why? Money? Some sort of loyalty? Quid pro quo? Crevecoeur could be playing him, Smith, Da Turtle, the Agency, or all three (or more, this being Haiti). It was a nut he would have to crack . We also, Smith mused to himself, lack the why. Why would a clandestine group be looking for rare earths? If it was a government, why clandestine and why Haiti? It would be a lot easier if they called this some sort of foreign aid project, bought the local elite and went on their nefarious way. This was getting too close to Spy-vs-Spy for comfort.

Smith poured himself a Scotch. The first thing we do is clear the human underbrush. Get rid of the wild men, he chuckled to himself, he had just caught himself humming an old Ian Whitcombe tune, "Where there are wild men, there must be wild women, so where did Robinson Crusoe go with Friday on Saturday night?" He must somehow isolate Da Turtle. His thoughts were interrupted by a call on his secure phone.

"Mr. Smith, you wanted us to trace the phone call from the Cap Haitian hotel to Key West?"

"Of course."

"We discovered the number in Key West. It went to a U.S. Coast Guard cutter. One other thing you might be interested in."

"Go ahead."

"The line had been tapped by someone more sophisticated than the Haitian police. We are running it down now, but whoever did the tapping is running a first class operation."

"Thank you. Keep me advised."

What the hell?

~ ~ ~

Da Turtle was watching *Better Call Saul* with his squinty testudinean eyes. He was convinced the television show had been based on him and he was making notes of similarities for a possible lawsuit. A few years ago he'd met the show's producer at a conference and perhaps he'd talked too freely over an expensive bottle of Bodegas Roda Cirsion.

Even so, Da Turtle found that he couldn't concentrate. It was a rare condition indeed for the sharply honed, Jesuit trained, three-pound brain that crowded his cranium. What was bothering him?

Then it came to him like Saul's epiphany on the road to Damascus – it was that damned woman. Moana Jones was trying to kill him. He didn't like that.

Da Turtle was a habitué of the 801 Club here in Key West. Most Sunday afternoons he could be found in the upstairs cabaret for another installment of gay bingo. He'd know Moana for nearly a dozen years and had met there, where she worked as a drag queen.

No, Da Turtle was straight as a pool stick. But he enjoyed the theatricality of it all: the drag queen calling out numbers, the audience shouting back like frenzied attendees at *The Rocky Horror Picture Show* ("Forty-two? You were forty-two twenty-nine years ago, Blanche!").

He always sat at the assigned Straight Table, even owned a T-shirt that warned DO NOT TEASE OR FEED THE STRAIGHT PEOPLE! But being a regular he'd come to know all the entertainers who dressed in women's clothing and exuded more femininity than most females.

Of course, "Moana Jones" was not the *faux femme fatale*'s real name. Neither was she Polynesian nor a reporter for the *International Herald Tribune*. Moana's street name was actually Monica – and she was one of Queen Mother Sushi's "girls."

Born Michael Fredric Jones, Monica was a curvy beauty, thanks to well-applied makeup, padded bra, and ultra-high heels. Monica was so expert at "hiding the candy," she'd often had hot, sweaty sex with men in the backseat of her car without them realizing the difference between closed thighs and a vagina.

Being a well-connected fixer, Da Turtle was aware that Monica Jones freelanced as an assassin, a profitable sideline that required little training or skills other than being able to aim and pull a trigger. However, it was quite clear Monica needed more practice, having missed him and hit that Coast Guard kid Lavon Perry.

Now that Da Turtle was back in the Conch Republic, on his own turf, he felt safer. But just to be sure, he decided to make a phone call to one of his posse, a man who could provide proper security for him.

Key West was a cauldron of intrigue and as such attracted an assortment of thugs, gamblers, druggies, con men, mercenaries, spies, attorneys and otherwise shady characters. Da Turtle knew them all.

~ ~ ~

Beach Parsons Jr. was a mercenary, and a good one. After cashiering out of the Army Special Forces, he'd hired out in Bosnia, Rwanda, the Congo, and El Salvador. But he had his standards; he wouldn't work for Arabs. They wiped their butts with their left hand. Beach had sanitary criterions.

Beach's father had been a four-star general, known for his bravery and tough demeanor. His son tried to live up to those standards, thus his career as a merc. Open for business, he had cards that proclaimed HAVE AR-15, WILL TRAVEL – a promotional item inspired by that old Western TV show starring craggy ol' Richard Boone.

Being the son of Gen. Beachard Parsons, he was often referred as "that son of a Beach." He didn't mind.

When Beach met Da Turtle at the Blue Macaw Bar in Key West, there was no hesitation in accepting the bodyguard assignment. The pay was good, he liked the wily Turtle, and he hadn't worked in three months, not since he'd help raid a treasure hunting ship. But as a hired hand, his take had been a mere fraction of a percent and he was already broke. His consumption of Mexican peyote was an expensive hobby.

"There's a simpler solution to your assassin problem,"

he told Da Turtle over a glass of 2008 Littoral Thieriot Vineyard Chardonnay.

"Such as?" Da Turtle, glanced around to make sure they were not being overheard. His head rotated like the girl in *The Exorcist.*

"Eliminate her. Nobody would object to one less 801 Club denizen."

"That's true. But I need to find out who hired Moana, I mean Monica. I have too many enemies to figure it out by going eeny-meeny-miny-moe."

"Shall I extract that information? A pair of pliers applied to well-manicured fingernails should do the trick."

"Not yet. She seems to be under the patronage of a ruddy Coast Guard officer. I'm not sure about the nature of that relationship."

"Yeah, I heard about that. She seems to have enchanted some big redheaded shallow water sailor. Does he know she's a he?"

"Beats me. I heard she cajoled him into a quickie marriage, but look for a hasty annulment when he tried to consummate it. He's gullible, but not gay according to all reports."

"I'd love to see that honeymoon video tape," chuckled Beach.

"For the time being, stick close to me and run interference. I've got a big deal going on and I don't need the distraction of a dick-dangling cross-dresser with a loaded gun."

"You got it, Boss," nodded that son of a Beach.

~ ~ ~

Da Turtle's wild ride on the Caterpillar D6 through the tangled jungle brush of *Vallée Mystérieuse* hadn't lasted long; just long enough to unearth a shallow formation of blue-green stone, its iridescence contrasting starkly with the black loam overlaying that rocky deposit. As soon as his devoted minions had crushed and gathered enough of the luminous mineral to fill a dozen barrels, Da Turtle was airlifted out of the jungle and once again airborne, was en route to a remote Bahamian cay favored by his smuggler clients as an entrepot for shipments of square grouper. There, in a windowless hidden lab supervised by the Slav, a small cadre of former East German chemists painstakingly refined this rarest of rare earths, isolating small batches of a previously-undiscovered element that Da Turtle had dubbed "Insidium."

Generations of Maroons had engaged in ritual use of the rare mineral, keeping to themselves the secret of its unique properties. Lord Gorton Pimlico Blackstraw was the only outsider ever chosen to receive this sacrament. Repeated consumption in the course of the Maroons' rituals had effected the remarkable changes that Blackstraw's fellow expatriates noted upon his lordship's return from the hidden valley. None of those gin-soaked wastrels connected the dots between his Lordship's indulgence in native rituals and his new persona, but that connection did not escape Da Turtle's unblinking glassy-eyed gaze. The opportunistic lawyer had seen fortunes being made by those who had chemically altered another native staple, the coca leaf, into cocaine. "Better living through chemistry," the reptilian barrister remarked to himself. So, he had wasted no time in locating, extracting and refining the Maroon's sacramental rock into a powder bursting with insidious potential. His secret laboratory refined a dozen barrels of ore into Insidium, one of which he then smuggled home to Key West aboard the Schooner Wolf.

"Why'd you give this stuff a Latin name?," Beach Jr. asked, when tasked with safeguarding Da Turtle 's Insidium stash.

"My friend, mastery of Latin enables one to relish the subtleties of scientific vocabulary. Here we have a sparkling turquoise dust whose benign appearance gives no hint of its profound psychotropic properties; a stealthy weapon in the right hands. To one schooled in etymology, this name brings to mind the Latin derivation of 'insidious', namely 'ambush'."

The Son of a Beach was well schooled in many useful

disciplines, etymology not among them. But he held an advanced degree in "ambush," acquired through intense studies at Mekong Delta U. He quickly grasped Da Turtle's meaning: this harmless —looking powder could be a weapon. "Insidium," indeed.

"How do you deliver it?" the mercenary inquired.

"That will depend on its intended use," Da Turtle replied. "A low dose endows one with exceptional attributes; but administered in a concentrated form, it induces violent aggressive behavior, very useful when directed against an unwary target. I will be marketing it for the latter purpose under the trademark 'Damnitol', but first I'll have to come up with labeling verbiage that's vague and misleading enough to avoid disclosing the occasional unfortunate side-effect, fatal psychosis. Evading FDA scrutiny is a challenging game these days."

Notwithstanding their very different backgrounds and professions , Beach and Da Turtle were a well matched pair. Others might characterize their shared outlook as cynicism, but they preferred realism; a personal philosophy untainted by morality or a misguided faith in human nature. When confronted with an obstacle, each instinctively responded with an effective, if amoral, countermeasure, to which Da Turtle customarily added a dash of deviousness. Neither felt compelled to engage in the formalities of polite society, except when dealing with restaurant staff (unwise to risk poisoning by a disgruntled chef or waiter). But Da Turtle's account of his Insidium scheme revealed to Beach a degree of cold calculation so extreme that no standard-issue thermometer could measure it. Beach wavered between awe and revulsion; awe won out. A fervent Hemingway fan, Beach recalled Martha Gelhorn's left-handed compliment of her ex-husband: "A man must be a very great genius to make up for being such a loathsome human being." Like Beach's literary idol, Da Turtle was both a genius and loathsome. It was sufficient for Beach.

~ ~ ~

After compressing the power and securing the Insidium

in a large First Florida National Bank safe deposit box, Beach returned to the Chart Room Bar to resume his conversation with Da Turtle.

To a visitor, the Chart Room would seem an unlikely venue for criminal conspiracy. It was the favorite watering hole of the State Attorney, the Sheriff , and the ancient Federal Judge, as well as a motley collection of local characters on both sides of the law. But no worries; adherence to an unspoken "Gentlemen's Code," prevailed. Nothing anyone might let slip there would be used against him, and (unlike some other Key West bars), you wouldn't find yourself in the midst of a fistfight between drunken shrimpers.

Da Turtle had limited the scope of Beach's assignment, for the moment at least,-to bodyguard service and safeguarding the Insidium stash. Finding out who had hired Moana, and eliminating the wannabe assassin, could wait 'til later . There were too many eyes on him. He had learned through a wiretap conducted by his Haitian allies that the Coast Guard officer, Le Gran Rouge, who apparently served as Moana's patron, was on a ship tied up in Key West harbor. Some government spook was also reportedly sniffing about. And then there was that corrupt cop, Cassamayor, who would be demanding answers about his nephew, Levon. It was a good time for Da Turtle to keep his head safely tucked into his shell until his carefully-planned scheme came to fruition.

~ ~ ~

"Good morning sir," was the salutation that greeted Da Turtle as he entered his office. It was but a brief respite from the usual Lewis-gun staccato of the typewriters at work in this sanctuary of efficiency. "Well-oiled machine" does not begin to describe the efficacy of this staff. He paid well, and expected nothing less than the best from his minions, with the added expectation that they possess tongues like the grave. "Yes," was his response as he moved on to his inner office, with barely the pause that one would attribute to a semicolon.

Once seated at his desk, he commenced with daily ritual of organizing all the correspondence that had accumulated on this sacred alter. This task complete, he rang for the lead clerk.

"Please to bring me the Charitable Trust file if you would be so kind," was his request to the trim, smartly-dressed woman that stood before him. "Oh, Oho, (that was her name,) and would you please prepare that document for Mr. Beach's signature?"

"Already done," was her response." "I will bring it into you directly, and shall I contact Mr. Beach and request him to drop by the office?"

"Yes," was Da Turtle's curt reply as he lowered his head in a sign of dismissal.

Once alone, Da Turtle turned round slowly in his chair and gazed pensively out of the window. Gently caressing his chin, he turned over in his mind the numerous events of late, and was for the most part satisfied with the results of his labors. All was proceeding as planned, but there remained a few unknowns that he did not have time to unravel. Best to let them play out in due course and in their own time, was his decided course of action. His contemplation was interrupted by a noise at the office door, followed by the entrance of Beach Parsons.

"You looking for me?" queried the disheveled Mr. Beach.

"Take a seat." was Da Turtle's response. Beach flopped down hard in the proffered chair and was about to place his feet upon Da Turtle's desk when he stopped and thought better of it.

"I have a very important document I wish for you to sign," stated Da Turtle, as he rang through to the outer office. "With the stroke of this pen, my good Beach, you will be transformed from village scofflaw to benevolent philanthropist"

Scratching his head with a puzzled look, Beach inquired of the lawyer, "Tell me again about this charity business."

"It's a Charitable Trust, my dear boy and you are going

to be its head," answered Da Turtle.

"Why me?" queried Beach.

The attorney cracked a smile, then posed a question, "Answer me this, if one wishes to hide a leaf one needs a forest; if one does not have a forest at hand, then we are compelled to make one, right?"

Beach slowly nodded his head in agreement. Da Turtle smiled and continued, "The Trust will prove an excellent place to both hide and distribute my Insidium."

Before he could proceed further, the door opened and the smartly-dressed clerk entered with the aforementioned document in hand. "Ready for your signature, Mr. Beach," she smiled.

Beach took the document from the clerk, a fountain pen from Da Turtle, and dutifully signed his name in all the designated places.

Upon completion of the last signature, Da Turtle retrieved his pen and the clerk lifted the paper and quietly withdrew from the room.

"Not so difficult was it?" inquired Da Turtle.

Beach shifted uneasily in his chair, a puzzled expression on his face. "What are we going to do with this Insidium stuff?" he asked Da Turtle .

"Make a fortune, of course," was Da Turtle 's curt reply.

"You already have a fortune," Beach shot back.

"Not large enough," responded Da Turtle. "Beach, you must understand that at the root of all great men and their fortunes lies a bank," the attorney continued. "This Insidium, which acts in the shadowlands of who men are, and who they wish to be, will provide me with the necessary capital to fund and control my own bank," gushed Da Turtle.

"Well, if you say so," mused Beach.

Da Turtle was about to continue when the phone rang. "Yes, OK, send him through," was his response, and placing the phone down, smiled at his friend and informed him that his favorite member of the police force was about to join their conversation.

Cassamayor burst into the office with all the noise of the circus come to town. Da Turtle, having much experience with this type, quickly seated him and directed him to get to the point.

"I want the lowdown on Lavon," he demanded abruptly. "But before you start, I have to give you this," said the policeman as he handed Da Turtle a calling card. Engraved upon the card were three initials that the lawyer recognized immediately. He said nothing, but turned and faced the window.

"What is it?" Cass and Beach asked, tension bubbling in their voices.

Da Turtle did not turn and face his two companions when he finally broke the deepening silence. "Because I could not stop for Death, he kindly stopped for me," sighed the emotionally shelled one and after a pause mentioned the name Emily Dickinson. "Emily who?" exclaimed the cop, "she a Conch?"

"No, man," Beach rolled his eyes and laughed, "she lives out in New Town."

"Emily Dickinson, is a conch?" Detective Cassamayor's dismal attempt at intellectual accomplishment dropped to the floor and flopped once, like a netted mullet resigned to his fate.

Beach Parsons left Da Turtle's office and headed for damp stench of stale peanuts, cheap cigars and dutiful politicians in the Chart Room Bar.

After a few beers and more than a few lies, Beach walked home to his cigar maker's cottage on Nassau Lane. He called it "my Beach house"! Because Beach had no porch light, he eventually located his hidden key; it was still in the door lock ... and stepped into a wooden box that creaked with every move. Beach opened a bottle of *Fouilly Puisse* and located his autographed copy of Emily Dickinson's collected poems which, according to the book dealer was, "Quiet rare."

Stirred by Da Turtle's final remarks, Beach vigorously thumbed through the moldy hardback and found the remains of the first troubling stanza.

> *Because I could not stop for Death-*
> *He kindly stopped for me-*
> *The carriage held but just Ourselves-*
> *And Immortality"*

It was the word Immortality that gave him pause. Immortality, what could be more appealing and addictive, especially to well-heeled old farts in their gold-plated dotage, than the thought of immortality?

He sat back and rolled a fatty to assist in contemplation of his recent employment.

Beach was reminded of people who, in their own mind, thought they were doing good even while doing bad. To a person, they had one thing in common, a way to describe the satellite influences in their life that gave valid reason to misbehave. Their logical insanity, combined with accommodating laws caused me to wonder if there were any guilty parties left on earth, were we running out of remorseful people?

Toke. Pause. Toke.

Even unscrupulous geniuses, and Da Turtle is a genius of sorts, have unobserved and therefore unprotected chinks in their felonious armor. After all the forethought, irksome references and familiar legal theater of pen, paper and pomp Beach had just been subjected to, he was amused, but not surprised to see that neither Da Turtle nor his minion had bothered to look closely at his signature. Blessed by the U.S. government, in days gone by, with three first-class sets of false identification papers, he had quickly learned to disguise his signature. Da Turtle's lack of attention to such detail was unusual and bothered him. Was Da Turtle losing his grip? Da Turtle knew Beach was right-handed because of where he carried my gun, but had he failed to notice Beach signing with his left hand?

After twenty-five years dealing with bad guys, the kind of guys who go around pissing on the snow drift of humanity, Beach was nonetheless surprised at their innate ability to fuck things up.

71

When Beach turned the page, the ash gave way and crashed onto the adjacent sheet. A scorching seed fell into the binding crotch and a miniature smoke plume was sucked upwards by my slow turning ceiling fan.

I focused and read the words adjacent to the smoking hole:

"A face devoid of love or grace,
A hateful, hard, successful face,
A face with which a stone
Would feel as thoroughly at ease
As were they old acquaintances-
First time together thrown."

This pulse of words reminded Beach both of Da Turtle (whose real name is Earl Nougat Esq.) and his dad, General Beachard Parsons III who given the spirit predictably quipped at inappropriate moments, "You don't know what the horse is going to do, until get on him and open the gate … Giddy the Fuck Up!" Why his brain combined these two thoughts he do not know.

Toke

After two years of attendance at Miss Rhonda Bordeleon's School of Social Dance and Virtuous Intention in Arlington, Virginia (an off-book facility for FPS/Force Protections Specialist training) and then another three years of grim, low-pay duty with Special Operations in dark muddy countries controlled by dark, muddy idiots, Beach Parsons decided that if he was going to get killed for no good reason, he'd like to die in the black.

Beach found Da Turtle's nominal lack of morality refreshing and had agreeably continued their relationship, on and off, over many years, continents, time zones, assassins and sweet scented Titty bars. Nor did he mind sitting second chair to the terrapinish scoundrel, under calm conditions preferably, since it presented the opportunity to observe the first chair and his doings, while giving Beach the split second opportunity to get off a few rounds and thin the herd before all hell broke loose.

Parsons knew Da Turtle was a wily fellow with the

compassionate demeanor of a river cat fish and the ferocity of a dry-humped mother beaver, but he usually got the deal done without troublesome complications or too much death and that, in their line of work, is considered success.

The fatty had famished from lack of dedicated inhalation, but the wine remained, prepared to console and help him ponder what glyphic Da Turtle had seen on the card Cassamayor gave him. Beach couldn't see the calling card and didn't want to be rude and ask, but whatever it was, it nearly caused Da Turtle to change his expression. His guess was either a new porn site or a death threat, neither of which prevented Parsons from falling asleep and dreaming how ripples from a pebble tossed into a pond looked like an ever expanding bull's eye.

~ ~ ~

Smith was finishing up a meeting with his new French counterpart. His old counterpart was old in both senses of the term, familiar and too advanced in age for field work. The new guy was sharp, energetic and a thorough professional. And, he was proving to be useful.

"Mr. Smith, I have the answer to a query you posed to my predecessor. He seemed to have put it in the wrong file, but I digress. I have some interesting information regarding a Moana Jones, the subject of an inquiry here. A French citizen of that name went missing ten years ago from a cruise ship that made a port call in Key West. A thorough search was made but she never re-boarded the ship. The authorities, both the FBI and local, made extensive inquiries, but they never located her. A cold case as you say until a warm body by the same name turned up in Haiti. Would you be able to shed some light for us?"

"How old was Jones when she disappeared?"

"Thirty-five."

"Positive?"

"Yes."

"That means that the present and missing Miss Jones aren't the same person, but there has to be a connection. Our Miss Jones has been making calls to Key West. The other one went missing there. Let me turn over some rocks. I'll keep you informed. Thanks."

"But of course."

Each went back to their respective embassies. Christ, Smith thought to himself, I'm beginning to hate Key West. Pigeons, Turtles, phone calls and now this. Then he had another thought, not a happy one. Tt seemed everyone was suddenly stepping up their game. But why? What kind of word was getting out about this hell-hole anyway?

Back at the French Embassy, the "Police Attaché" and the Ambassador were having a chat.

"Nice to have you here," said the Ambassador. "I specifically asked for you once I recognized our good friend Smith. He is a very senior, very experienced agent and a hard case. Normally someone like that would be running a major operation, never a third-tier assignment like Haiti. The Americans are up to something. Our communications people picked up some strange transmissions from a valley north-west of here. Open channel, probably commercial or criminal, probably not government. If this is an intelligence operation, back away from it. If they want our help they'll ask. No point in interfering. But, if it is criminal or commercial, find out whatever is going on. Besides, if you stay close enough, the old dog might teach you some useful tricks. He didn't stay alive this long just by being lucky. Dismissed."

A few days later, Lt. Cassamayor was handed an old missing person's report and an INTERPOL request for assistance in providing any information on a French citizen, Moana Jones, who went missing in Key West ten years ago. Cassamayor took the report, mumbled something about needless paperwork, and walked back to his office and shut the door. He drew the blinds. Then he started to shake uncontrollably. He took half an hour to calm down enough to think clearly. Damn, he thought to himself, I knew this day was coming.

Ten years earlier he provided some unofficial but very profitable assistance to a drug smuggling ring that was employing cruise ship crewmen to move cocaine and heroin into the U.S. via Key West. Stand around, look, no heavy lifting. His kind of job. Then things went horribly wrong. A lookout spotted a woman with a pair of binoculars on the verandah of a hotel that overlooked the cruise ship pier. The woman, realizing that she had been spotted, tried to leave but didn't make it out of the hotel. A few hours later, Cassamayor was told to drive to the hotel's loading dock and pick up a package. When he got there a couple of large, menacing Slavic-sounding guys put a body-sized object covered in a plastic tarp in his trunk. His contact, a nasty Miami Cuban, told him to find somewhere out-of-the-way and bury it. No peeking, the Cuban told him. Just bury "it." He was also told something else – if anyone, anyone ever hears of this Cassamayor would have his balls cut off while he watched his family butchered. He took "it" to No Name Key and buried the package.

For the next few weeks the Feds rattled every cage looking for a missing woman named Moana Jones. Cassamayor got the feeling that this wasn't just a tourist they were looking for. In the process, the Feds scared up enough old dirt to convict most of the Key West Police Department and half of the detectives in the Monroe County Sherriff's office of various offenses. Cassamayor lucked out, just. In any case, "Moana Jones" was never located and things went back to normal, except that with his two superiors serving long Federal time, Cassamayor got a major promotion. The proverbial silver lining. Now Fate was back, and not happy. Cassamayor decided to look busy, something he was good at.

If he was going to stay ahead of whatever was happening, he needed to get in the middle and find out before anyone else did. So, he got to work. His informants told him that there was another "Moana Jones" and that she too was missing. Except, except – she wasn't a she, and he found where she, he, whatever was. And, he found out a few other things, too. Never doubt the example of violence, carefully applied.

A few hate crimes later, Cassamayor found out that "Moana Jones" was the trade name for a local drag queen. Said drag queen was now in Haiti. Even better, said drag queen was gunning, albeit not very accurately, for Da Turtle. God does have a sense of humor Cassamayor thought. He, Cassamayor, just didn't want to be the punch line in a divine joke. He couldn't believe it was a coincidence that the drag queen picked "Moana Jones" of all names. What did "Moana" know about "Moana"? How, and how much, did he find out? And, Cassamayor nearly retched when he thought it, how did Da Turtle get involved? Mercifully, he had eyes and ears headed to Haiti. Looking for Moana Jones no less and with a grudge against Da Turtle . Cassamayor headed to the Coast Guard base.

"Sir, a Lt. Cassamayor to see you."

"Thanks, I'll be right down." What now, I thought to myself?

I met Cassamayor at the quarterdeck and brought him up to my stateroom. I was packing to go to Haiti, so there wasn't a place to sit down.

"Don't mean to be inhospitable Cass. What can I do for you?"

"I need to tell you a few things before you go," he said.

"Such as?"

"How well do you know your wife?"

"We aren't married" I told him, "yet."

"Hold that thought. Have you been, err, ah, intimate?"

"Are you from the Health Department?"

"No."

"Her family?"

"No."

"Are you doing research, because you don't look like either Masters or Johnson?"

"No."

"Then WTF?"

"She looks like a she but isn't she."

"What is black and bigger than a breadbox?"

"What?"

"The God damned bowling ball I'm going to stuff down your throat! Why the questions."

"I'd love to see the look on your face when you found out, but I thought I'd spare you the shock" Cassamayor said. "She is a he and with him you don't want to be, unless you do but I don't think so."

I nearly puked, from embarrassment if nothing else. People have committed suicide for lesser things.

"This is still an opportunity. Find out what the hell is going on down there, because there is an obvious connection to Key West, and I want to know what it is. Besides, this is another nail in the Da Turtle's coffin." Cassamayor smiled.

"So, we are going from a rescue to a fishing expedition. Still," I said "if this can help me to find out why Lavon was shot, I'll do it."

"Good man. Pack and let me know when you get to Haiti."

"Will do," I said.

Cassamayor left. I needed a drink, then I thought better of it. Wasn't enough rum on the planet to wash this off. Don't start what you can't finish. What the hell was I thinking? Then I went back to packing.

Cassamayor was suddenly in a better mood.

Smith was in his office when he picked up a message from the secure communications room. The technical branch had done an analysis of material retrieved from a Coast Guard boarding of a dilapidated schooner headed for – no, no, wait, don't tell me – thought Smith. Key West. Now I officially hate the place. The material looked like common dirt. The Coast Guard boarding officer thought it was odd that a boat en route to Key West from Haiti would be carrying a cargo of dirt. He got suspicious when the crew got agitated and demanded it back. What was in the dirt, he thought, so he had it sent to a forensic lab. Smith had read the report – anything going to or from Haiti was now important – so he had the material tested in a lab attached to the intelligence community.

The analysis confirmed that the material was a particularly rare, rare, earth but the lab wouldn't even guess as to potential applications. The dirt went to MIT. Someone with time on his hands had done some research and, voila, the application revealed itself. The report said that the rare earth was used by native healers in Haiti to revive zombies. No other known references.

"Heal the sick, raise the dead, drive the little girls right out of their heads." Smith told himself he had to stop listening to Miami AM stations. Still, the lyrics got him thinking. What was a zombie? A semi-dead person. What did this stuff do, again? It came to him. At the very least, this stuff probably stopped the appearance of the aging process. Wonder what the FDA would think of a CIA demand for extensive consumer testing – first Ralph Nader, now a bunch of spooks – not something that happened every day. Then things really started to fall into place.

First, this was a private commercial venture. That explained the pigeons, open channel communications and the person-to person graft as opposed to some sort of inflated foreign aid packages with a big foot print. Low budget, low visibility. That also explained the not-so-guided bullets whizzing by. Established secret services rarely killed their professional opposite numbers. They offed informants and sources certainly, but fellow members of the club? Private ventures are much more inclined to public violence.

Secondly, if this was a private venture, that would explain the haphazard infrastructure. Whoever was behind this didn't need to produce much of anything. All they needed to do was demonstrate that they could if they chose to. What he was up against was an elegant shakedown scheme Smith thought to himself. All the time he was thinking about a hostile government securing sole access to a strategically vital commodity. This bunch had found the rarest of rare earths. It wasn't good for anything, anything that is, except keeping the appearances of age at bay. No government would give much of a damn. Then it really hit him.

78

Who was being shaken down? He picked up the phone and buzzed the embassy's economic attaché. Here is a guy with time on his hands Smith thought – an economic attaché in a country without an economy. Time he had something to do.

"Hello, this is Mr. Smith, the RSO. I have a request for you."

"How can I help you?" the attaché asked. Normally he would have made a snide comment about such a request being beneath his dignity, but he had noticed that the Ambassador came to Smith, not the other way around. Smith probably didn't do snide.

"I need you to find out what the world market in anti-aging products is worth."

"When do you need an answer?"

"Tomorrow morning."

"But it's Friday night. I have plans for the weekend." He knew he had just said something stupid.

"As of now your plans consist of working tonight, tomorrow and however long it takes to get me my answer. Ever lived in Mongolia?"

"You have made yourself very clear, sir. I'm on it."

"Good." Smith smiled to himself. It was a source of personal pride that he could terrify people without even raising his voice.

Smith knew he was on to something. Someone, probably that damned Turtle, was holding the cosmetics industry hostage. Their profit streams, advertising, production facilities and especially, their aura of authority, was up in smoke if the secret was out. All he had to so was send them a bottle of pills, cream, whatever it was, and the numbers to an off-shore account, and wait. He poured himself a Scotch, sat down and congratulated himself on a job well done. Then he shot upright. Well done, hell. Wait a minute. What would a multi- billion, multi-national industry do when threatened with extinction? The British and Americans had done some nasty things for their respective oil companies. If you can destabilize governments in the name of Imperial Oil or Standard Oil, why not Estee Lauder? That would explain the sudden improvement in the quality of his foreign colleagues. France, China and the UK all had huge cosmetics industries. They had gone to their respective governments for help. That is how the word had gotten out about Haiti. Life was going to get interesting. Soon. As if on cue his phone rang. The call was from the Marine security detail.

"Sir, we have four of the biggest human beings I have ever seen in my life. They are covered in tattoos, even their faces. Oh, and sharpened teeth. One is carrying what looks like a shark-tooth headed war club. They all say they are from Bora-Bora and they are looking for a Moana Jones. Would you come down and talk to them, because I'm sure as hell not letting them into the building."

"On my way." Smith hung up the phone. When I thought soon, I meant soon, not instantaneous, Smith mused to himself. First a Da Turtle, now cannibals, I can't believe I get paid for this.

~ ~ ~

Prosper Saint Robards looked very threatening in his black suit, black hat, and black-as-midnight sunglasses. He and his partner Moufon were agents of the *Milice de Volontaires de la Sécurité Nationale*. This was the official name of the Tonton Macoute, the spécial operations unit created in 1959 by François "Papa Doc" Duvalier as a paramilitary force that reported only to the self-proclaimed "President for Life."

When Duvalier died in 1971, he was succeeded by his son Jean-Claude "Baby Doc" Duvalier. The Tonton Macoute continued its clandestine role. The nickname came from a mythological Haitian boogeyman known as Uncle Gunnysack. This monster was said to snare bad children in a sack and carry them away to be eaten for breakfast. In a similar way, the Ton-Ton made people disappear for political reasons. Or simply for fun.

Prosper and Moufon had been assigned to stop the theft of a rare earth that had regenerative properties. It was widely used by Vodou priests to reanimate dead bodies. Many Ton-Ton Macoute were *Vodou* followers. The ore was mined in *Vallée Mystérieuse*, a gorge near the mountainous Dominican Republic border.

They had traced a shipload of this *saleté spéciale* to Key West, that island at the ass-end of Florida. Certain informants – *informateurs confidentiels*, as they were known within the Police Nationale d'Haïti. The PNH had very good sources, reaching even into the French Embassy, Interpol, and the U.S. Coast Guard.

According to a source close to a big ruddy-faced Coast Guard officer named Smith, the beefy redhead was hot on the trail of the *saleté spéciale*. Prosper's *informateur confidentiel* reported that Smith suspected a shadowy character known as Da Turtle. But no one could figure out Da Turtle's game. Known as a "fixer," *Monsieur Tortue* was a difficult man to pin down.

Prosper figured that he and Moufon could snatch *Monsieur Tortue* and extract any necessary information before making him permanently disappear. The Ton-Ton Macoute was good at that.

Making people talk was not much of a challenge. Moufon simply chopped off a subject's fingers, one by one, with his machete, until they got the information they sought. Moufon enjoyed interrogating people. He was called *Le Hachoir*, the Chopper.

The Ton-Ton agents had traced *Monsieur Tortue* to Key West, his homeport. That meant they must travel there to "interview" him. However, that presented a problem. Word was *Monsieur Tortue* had hired a bodyguard, a merc named Beachard Parsons Jr.

Beach Parsons was known to Prosper. He had once crossed paths with this self-styled "Son of a Beach." The merc was *fou dans la tete*. The crazy bastard had no fear of the Ton-Ton Macoute, no fear of Voodoo *bokors*, no fear of death.

It was said that Beach Parsons carried at least six deadly weapons on him at all times. Not counting his trusty

AR-15, the 45-calibre M1911 tucked in his shoulder holster, a snub-nosed S&W .38 in an ankle holster, a 7" fixed blade SOG SEAL 2000 knife strapped to his thigh, a *shuriken* hand blade in his left-hand trouser pocket, a fake fountain pen that squirted cyanide in his shirt pocket, and a belt buckle that disguised a sharp 3" blade/bottle opener. This didn't even count the toothpick he chewed on, a deadly weapon when poked into an eyeball, penetrating the brain. Beach Parsons was a walking arsenal.

~ ~ ~

Prosper Saint Robards and his partner arrived at Key West Municipal Airport that rainy September day in 1983. A hurricane was hovering south of Cuba, threatening the Florida Keys. He and Moufon had caught one of the last flights out of Miami.

They were traveling in disguise. Both wore flowery tropical shirts and Bermuda shorts, posing as calypso singers. The *Milice de Volontaires de la Sécurité Nationale* had secured them a gig at Cecil's 21 Club in Bahama Village. Prosper had a pretty good voice, but Malfor sounded like a bullfrog getting gutted.

They had smuggled their pistols, two Al-Qadissiya Tariq semi-automatic pistols, Iraqi-produced knockoffs of the classic Beretta M1951, inside a conga drum. The cartons of 7.65mm parabellum cartridges had been secreted in a bongo drum. Custom agents showed little interest in musical instruments being shipped in the plane's cargo hold.

Their passports said they were from Jamaica. Nobody paid close attention. Musicians, smugglers, tourists, and spies came and went with a degree of impunity. Ever since the recent Conch Republic rebellion, the Florida Keys were enjoying an open-door policy.

The sun was like a dried-up mango in the morning sky, the heat evaporating the sweat on Prosper's skin and leaving a crust of salt. The rain had cleared up, a reprieve from the impending hurricane. He was happy to be away from Port-au-Prince, a dismal city wallowing in poverty.

Fortunately, the MSVN had given him and Malfor a special budget for this assignment. The taxi from the municipal airport to Duval Street alone cost $10, nearly a third of the average Haitian's annual income. Prosper felt he was living like a king.

"Disappearing" *Monsieur Tortue* would not be easy. First they had to take out that son of a beach bodyguard. However, that might be a challenge. It was said he had eyes in the back of his head – like the eight-eyed jumping spider. A tricky adversary indeed.

As Prosper and Moufon unloaded their bags and drums from the taxi, they did not notice the beautiful Eurasian woman standing in the shadows outside of Sloppy Joe's. She eyed them carefully. Her "fiancé" had let it slip that the Ton-Ton Macoute had set its sights on Da Turtle . So she was there to greet the two assassins.

Question was, since they shared the same goal, were the Haitians allies or interference? Should she make contact, join forces with them? Or take them out, maintaining fewer pieces on the chessboard?

Making up her mind to a course of action, Moana stepped from the shadows and said in flawless French, "Hello, boys. Looking for a good time?" *"Salut les gars. Vous cherchez un bon moment?"*

Across the street, Capt. Tony Tarracino was standing in front of his yellow-fronted saloon. Like infallible radar, he spotted the looker in front of Sloppy Joe's. "Hotcha," he muttered to himself and made a beeline to where she stood with the two men.

"Hold on, doll," he rasped. "You don't want to get involved with these two spooks. Come over to my saloon and I'll buy the drinks. I got a weakness for exotic women. And you make my knees weak."

Moana paused, her hand in her bag, fingers curled around the Walther PPK. "Don't bother me, old man," she snapped. "I am talking to my friends."

Spooks? thought Prosper Saint Robards. *How did he know we are spies?* "Come," he whispered to Malfor. "We must get away from this man. Take only your drum."

"Wait! *Reviens-moi!*" the woman called after the fleeing Haitians. But they had more resolve than Lot's wife, not bothering to look back as they headed in the general direction of Bahama Village.

Capt. Tony plastered a broad smile on his wrinkled face. "Let 'em go, honey. You an' me got drinkin' to do."

"Get lost, you old *fou.*"

"Don't be so hasty, sugar tits. I'm on my fourth wife. You could be number five."

"*Dans un oeil de cochon,*" she spat. "Congratulate yourself, old man. You saved their worthless lives."

"Forget it," he muttered, heading back across the street toward his saloon. "Damn females, always talking gibberish."

~ ~ ~

Moana Jones stood there on the hot sidewalk, steaming with anger. She was trying to decide whether to chase after the two men, or head back to the 801 Club. Sushi had her booked for the early evening show. She would be singing "I'm in Love with a Wonderful Guy," a show tune from Roger and Hammerstein's *South Pacific*. It was always a crowd pleaser with gay members of the audience. She enjoyed entertaining folks almost as much as she like being a paid assassin. On second thought, killing people paid better than working as a drag queen.

Martin Jones had come to Key West to search for his missing mother. She'd disappeared from a cruise to this tiny port ten years ago. Using her name was a way, he hoped, of drawing out the person or persons responsible for her disappearance. Bait, as it were. Working as a drag queen at the 801 got the name out there to the public. He/she had taken up working as an assassin out of boredom. This was such a sleepy little island.

Lost in these thoughts, Moana did not notice the tall man wearing a bush hat who stepped around the corner, his SOG SEAL 2000 knife concealed in his hand. She sensed his presence at the last moment, whirling to face the stealthy man and muttering, "Son of a Beach," or words to that effect.

With a quick flick of his SOG SEAL, Beach slit the sultry slut's dress from navel to neck. Moana leaped back, but Beach's blade had done its work, exposing the plastic tits fronting the faux female's formidable but phony physique. "As I suspected, a 'bini boy,'" Beach exclaimed (thus revealing his service-related familiarity with the treacherous he-she Pilipino B "girls" of Olongapo). Stripped of his false front, Martin/Moana fled in disgrace and a trail of mascara, shedding wig and heels in haste to escape public pudendal pruning at the hand of that mercenary S.O.B.

~ ~ ~

The cop on duty was knocking back a shot of buchi when Moana burst into the undistinguished '50s CBS building on Angela St. that housed City Hall, Fire House #1, Police HQ and the municipal jail. Sgt. "Mondo" Cabrera was unfazed by the sudden appearance of a frantic, partly-disrobed transvestite; the "girls" who plied the Pink Triangle were habitués of his booking desk. They often presented in a real or feigned state of panic, complaining of having been ripped off or bitch-slapped, or in custody for having committed one of the aforementioned offenses, or as a Signal 20 in need of temporary confinement until the drugs wore off. Cabrera's quick take on Moana's babbling about an assassin was "nut job," so the defrocked drag queen was unceremoniously dragged to the so-called padded cell (which lost its padding years ago when a local lunatic somehow managed to set it ablaze). While en route to her cell, the drag queen caught a glimpse of Prosper and Moufon being led in handcuffs to a holding cell, with Det. Lt. Cassamayor following closely.

On lower Duval St., two burly Haitian thugs in Bermuda shorts and Hawaiian shirts were as conspicuously incongruous as Liberace in a sumo wrestlers loincloth. Word of their presence spread rapidly over the Coconut Telegraph, reaching Cassamayor's ear within minutes after the Haitians' hasty departure from Sloppy Joe's. Moments later, a squad car carrying three of Key West's Finest apprehended the gaudy duo and their gun-laden drums on Whitehead St., and delivered them, manacled, to the Detective Lt.

"Seems you boys were planning to play something more explosive than 'Day-O' with these," Cass said, gesturing toward his captives' heavily-laden drums. When they responded with nothing more than menacing scowls, he turned toward Mondo Cabrera and tersely ordered: "Call Dr. Phibes."

~ ~ ~

Det. Sammy Lastres, a wiry 20-year veteran of the KWPD, whose hands were as quick as his ready wit, had earned the moniker "Dr. Phibes" by employing diabolical surgical skills. Whenever the cops threw a fat-walleted inebriated tourist into the drunk tank, the call would go out from KWPD Dispatch: "Dr. Phibes, you're wanted in surgery." So summoned, Lastres would appear at the jail forthwith, where he would perform a walletectomy, skillfully removing the drunken tourist's cash without awakening the passed-out "patient."

~ ~ ~

Having separated Prosper and Moufon from their drums, Cass put Lastres' skills to use. Dr. Phibes surgically removed the contents of the drums without damaging the instruments or the weapons hidden inside them. A quick inventory of the guns & ammo revealed that these were no common thugs; they were also sufficiently disciplined to remain silent in the face of standard police questioning. Cass grinned confidently; he'd soon have these "Calypso junkanoos" singing like Harry Belafonte. The Detective Lt. was a master of interrogation techniques more subtle than those favored by the Chopper, but equally effective. Without leaving a mark, he extracted from his captives the purpose and object of their Key West visit. "Hold them on suspicion of drumming up mayhem," he ordered Mondo. "They may prove useful."

Cass then turned his attention to the drag queen in the padded cell. Moana/Martin had calmed down after spending a few hours in a dank dark concrete box whose stark uniformity was relieved only by a hole in the center of the floor and a 6-inch square window in the door. Not the most welcoming accommodations, but at least Moana would be temporarily secure from the predations of that S.O.B. who had slashed her dress. The Drag Queen belatedly recognized the futility of undertaking to gun down the elusive and well-protected Da Turtle. Having explored every inch of the deep gulf separating artifice from reality, she grudgingly realized that her amateur "assassin" persona wouldn't stand a chance against a professional like Beach. Then, *deus ex machina*, Cass appeared at the window of the padded cell. After unlocking the cell door and bowing in mock obeisance to the disheveled Drag Queen, he led Moana through the jail to the parking lot outside. With a sweeping gesture toward his unmarked unit, he announced in an exaggerated baritone: "Princess, your pumpkin awaits."

"You are going to have to sit in the back. Department policy, but I can give you a ride,"

The bedraggled drag queen got into the car. Cassamayor got behind the wheel and started the car. He also locked the doors and windows before he backed out of the parking lot.

"You mind telling me why you use "Moana Jones" as your trade name?"

"Why do you want to know?"

"Ten years ago I looked for a missing person by that name. Moana isn't a common name down here. Looked high and low, with a lot of federal help. Never found her. Not a trace. Now a second "Moana Jones" shows up. Don't tell me it's a coincidence."

"It isn't."

"So, answer my question."

"I was ten when my mother disappeared. She was a detective in the French national police, narcotics and international crime. She was looking into a narcotics ring that was using cruise ships to smuggle drugs from the Caribbean to France. She disappeared in Key West or so my dad told me."

"You're French?"

"Dual nationality. My father was American."

"Was?"

"He died three years ago."

"What did he do?"

"He worked for the State Department. That is how they met. No family now except for an uncle I never met and my grandfather. My uncle works for the government but no one can tell me where or how. My grandfather is a tribal chief in Polynesia. That is where my mom was from and why she left. He is real traditional. Old religion, old ways. Mom just couldn't cope and went to school in France rather than stay out there. Tattoos, war clubs, ritual cannibalism for all I know. Met him once. Scared hell out of me and everyone else at the airport. Never said a word. Never had to."

Throughout the conversation Cassamayor kept driving. He was now on South Roosevelt, passing the beach and clearly headed out of town. Martin/Moana noticed.

"Where the hell are you going. You passed my apartment. Let me the hell out."

"Little late for that. You gotta go."

"Why? What did I do to you?"

"Because you are a loose end and I can't afford loose ends. Nothing personal. Enjoy the rest of the trip."

Martin /Moana wanted to scream but he was in the back of a police car and knew that wasn't going to get him anywhere. He needed to think, hard and fast.

"Where are we going?"

"Up the Keys."

They were mid-way across the Saddlebunch Keys when a DC-3 flew low towards them, just clearing the power line and houses. Cassamayor nearly drove off the road. The plane banked and turned toward the Gulf, gaining altitude as it left.

"Useless pieces of shit. Spraying for bugs, my ass!"

"Who was that?"

"The Mosquito Control airplane. Old fighter jocks that fly ancient crates at the public expense. They'd use Sopwith Camels if they could find some. Pretend they were the Red Baron. Scare hell out of everybody. End up landing in someone's roof."

Martin/Moana didn't see anything coming out of the airplane except engine oil, but kept that thought to himself.

"I'm a loose end. I just met you. Loose end of what"

"Loose end to a get-rich-quick scheme come back to bite me in the ass. Right people find out about you wrong things happen to me and mine. Sorry about your Momma. Right place, wrong time."

"You killed my mother?"

"No, but I know who did. Not nice people. They find out that you can link me to them, I'm dead."

"I can't link you to anybody. Thanks for the ride. Let me out and you'll never see me again."

"Nice try. Either you're dead or I am. I choose you."

Cassamayor turned left on Big Pine Key. A black Ford Crown Victoria passed in the other direction, then turned into a store parking lot. Cassamayor was talking and didn't notice the car turning around.

"Where are we going?"

"No Name Key. A great place...if you can find it, or so they say. Look on the bright side. You'll have lots of company. It's the local out-of-the-way place."

Cassamayor didn't mention that Martin/Moana might meet his mother there.

Passing a ramshackle fishing camp, Cassamayor drover the bridge to No Name. Another half mile and he stopped by a stand of Australian Pines. Leaving Martin/Moana in the car he headed for the trees. Then he stopped and nearly screamed. There was an open, grave sized hole where he had buried "it" years ago. Hole, no body sized package in it. What the hell? No one saw him when he buried the package, "it."

Cassamayor looked up to see the DC-3 make a low pass over the island. The plane's racket masked the noise of the car pulling in behind his. A few seconds later someone he didn't see stuck a hypodermic needle in his neck.

~ ~ ~

Cassamayor woke up. He had no idea where he was or how long he had been out. His last memory was looking up at a plane, then what was likely a needle in his neck. He tried to orient himself. He was sitting in a high-backed chair. He tried to move but couldn't. He couldn't feel his body. He was facing a raised dais. He was in a courtroom! What the hell? As his vision became less blurry he became more confused. This was like no courtroom he had ever seen before. There were two flags, one on either side of the judge's chair. Emblazoned on one were two crossed pitchforks. The other had two lightning bolts over the motto: "Bad day to be you." There was an enormous TV screen next to the dais. The emblem on the judge's bench was a women holding a scale in her right hand. On the scale were what looked like two testicles. The middle finger on her left hand was raised in all-too-familiar gesture. She was wearing a sash with the words "hell hath no fury like a woman scorned." Behind him he heard a voice announce "All rise, the honorable Max E. Roach presiding."

He tried to stand up, but couldn't. As he watched an enormous insect, dressed in a judges' gown, entered the room and took his seat. "Take your seats please" said the insect/judge. "Are we ready to proceed?" he asked. Cassamayor's chair swiveled. He was now facing a seven foot tall parrot. "Yes, your honor, the prosecution is ready" the parrot told the insect. Cassamayor's chair swiveled again. He as facing what looked like four enormous men in gorilla suits or four gorillas with good posture, he couldn't decide which. The largest gorilla rose and addressed the insect in an odd accent "the jury is ready, your honor." The chair swiveled again. Cassamayor was now looking at the insect. "Is the defense ready?" asked the insect. Cassamayor managed to croak "I want a lawyer." "Of course," replied the insect. " Quite correct." From behind Cassamayor's right shoulder a tentacle placed a framed picture of the Chief Justice of the United States next to his chair. "Let the record show that the defendant has been provided with a lawyer" said the insect. "That's not a lawyer" screamed Cassamayor. "Are you suggesting that the Chief Justice isn't a lawyer?" asked the insect. "Objection overruled." "You can't do that" shouted Cassamayor. "I'm your imagination, I can do whatever I like" replied the insect. "And, by the way, you will address me as "Your Honor."

The parrot spoke up. "The defendant is charged with various crimes of omission and commission which have led to a lifetime's perversion of justice. He has prostituted justice but now demands her protection. Protection denied. He has pled guilty to all charges. We are here merely to ascertain the severity of the sentence."

"I didn't plead to anything, and I still want a lawyer. What do you think I am, chopped liver?" demanded Cassamayor."

"Perhaps you are," replied the smiling insect. "The court will consider your statement. In the meantime, consider yourself guilty – and provided with a lawyer."

"Yes, your honor," Cassamayor caught himself saying.

The Parrot took the floor. "I direct your attention to the following recorded interviews. In each case the defendant freely admits his guilt." The television flashed on. Hours and hours of testimony in which Cassamayor pleaded guilty to a host of crimes, providing expletive laced, detailed descriptions of his actions, his opinions of victims, fellow policemen, wife, children, parents, city leaders, lawyers and judges. He described in detail his relationship with a host of criminal organization, naming names, providing numbers to off-shore bank accounts, the amounts he had stolen, been paid or favors granted over a twenty five year career in Key West law enforcement. In a concluding statement he looked directly into the camera, smiled and said "and fuck them all – come and get me."

At the conclusion, a visibly weary insect looked over to

the jury. "Gentlemen, have you reached a decision?"

"We have, your honor" replied the largest gorilla.

"What then say you," asked the insect.

The gorilla stood and took off his head, revealing a heavily tattooed human face with sharpened teeth. "We find the defendant guilty of being a piece of chopped liver," replied the gorilla / man.

"Thank you for your service," replied the insect. The insect then looked at Cassamayor. "You are hereby sentenced to be taken to a place of consumption, where you will be eaten by the jury. May God have mercy on your soul, as I will have none." Cassamayor looked down. His body had been marked like a beef carcass, labelling his body parts "steak, "roast," "loin," "liver."

"You can't do this!" screamed Cassamayor.

"You weren't listening," said the insect. "I am your imagination. I can do anything." Cassamayor fainted.

Cassamayor shook his head and opened his eyes. He was in the bottom of a hole looking up at a crowd of faces. The faces were connected to a group of Monroe County Public Works workers making their annual appearance outside of Key West. "Well, if it isn't our favorite TV star," said the foreman. "Dave, call the sheriff."

"Don't bother" said Cassamayor, "I'm fine."

"The hell you are," said the foreman, who then pointed to Cassamayor and started to laugh. Cassamayor looked down. He was naked, and his body had been marked like a beef carcass. He fainted.

Cassamayor later found out that his "testimony" had been televised, someone with a great deal of technical sophistication had placed different segments on the local Miami news programs without the station's knowledge or consent. What resulted was a local, then regional, then a national sensation. His "confessions" became prime time required watching. He could never remember what had happened or who had taped him. He could never forget the trial, either.

He was taken into custody while a judge determined

whether or not his "confessions" were admissible in court. While in custody he learned that a Cuban narcotics gang had imploded, resulting in several gruesome deaths, the Key West PD was the target of an intensive Federal and State investigation – again, and that his now destitute wife was filing for divorce. She had been admitted into the witness protection program and had been moved to Cody, Wyoming, an unimaginable place for a fifth-generation Conch who had never been further than Stock Island in her life.

"When did you know you hated your mother" asked his court-appointed psychiatrist?

"I don't," replied Cassamayor.

"Listen up," said the doctor, "you don't have much time. If you want to be cured we had better hurry."

~ ~ ~

Smith was getting on the morning American Airlines flight from Miami to Port au Prince. He had asked for a week's leave to take care of "old family business" and was returning to his embassy assignment. He shook hands with a younger man.

"I should have kept in touch. My wife was sick and I didn't have the time. When she died I just checked out. Sorry. Glad you got to meet your grandfather. Interesting gentleman. Oh, and stay out of Haiti. I have no jurisdiction here. Do there. I will have the locals bring you in for shooting that kid. Family or not. Lucky for you I found out you had flown back to Key West and followed you. Leave town. Go somewhere else. Now. Stay out of my sight."

About the same time four enormous, threatening looking, heavily tattooed Polynesian men boarded an Air France flight to Paris, then Tahiti. They were, they told the immigration officer, members of a Polynesian dance troupe that had been performing at the world famous Hukilau club in Key West. Had he been there?

~ ~ ~

I had just arrived in Key West from Haiti after two fruitless weeks of searching for Moana him/her. I had

93

wanted to find him/her/them. And I didn't want to. Did see one strange sight – what looked like a Polynesian war party talking to someone who was apparently a long-lost relative in front of the Embassy in Port-au-Prince. Lots of back slapping and nose rubbing. Even the Marines were backing off. Would not want to cross those gentlemen, dark alley or high noon. Anyway, unless I was researching my magnum opus, writing the definitive Third-World travel guide, I had wasted my time. Damn I was glad to get back. About three hours later, just as I was leaving the ship and headed tom the Chartroom Bar looking for an epic hangover, I was stopped at the Quarterdeck.

"Phone call for you, sir." The watch stander gave me an evil look. "Long distance, collect."

I felt like a hypocrite. Accepting collect phone calls on a government phone was an established no-no. I had lectured my troops about it and now here I was.

"Get the number, I'll call back from a phone on the pier."

"Yes sir."

A moment later the watch stander gave me a slip of paper with the number. I went down the pier to a public phone, pulled out my AT&T card and called. 206, Washington State, but I didn't recognize the number.

"I'm returning your call. To whom am I speaking?"

A familiar voice, only more male sounding this time, answered "I owe you an apology."

"Just one? Try again."

"Look, I'm sorry I shot your friend – an accident, and I'm sorry I let you make the, er, ah, assumptions you did. It wasn't personal."

"I feel so much better now," voice heavy with sarcasm, "What in hell was going on down there?"

"I came down here to smoke out whoever it was that killed my mother – long story. I was nearly killed by Cassamayor. Maybe you know him. He was working with a drug ring. They killed her. He covered it up. Here is what is important – your friend was Cassamayor's Godson. Lavon's

94

mother used to worked for Da Turtle . She and Da Turtle were having an affair. At least that is what people thought. Cassamayor found out. He had something else on them, no one else knows what. Perhaps Lavon did. That is why everyone at the hotel bar in Haiti was so interested when he spoke up. Half of them wanted to find out what he knew. The other half wanted him quiet. I have to go."

"Go to hell." The line went dead. I found out later the call was from am public phone booth in Laurier, Washington, an isolated border crossing into British Columbia. According the RCMP, a young woman crossed the border into Canada, but no women, only a non-descript looking young man, got on the only bus to Vancouver. No trace after that.

I was headed to a dry martini the size of a large swimming pool. Why was that crowd in Haiti when we were? What was going on between Lavon's mother, Cassamayor and the Da Turtle? Is that what got Lavon killed?

~ ~ ~

Da Turtle was breathing easier. The shipment of that material his Haitian partners called *saleté spéciale* was safely ensconced in a warehouse on Stock Island, one bridge up from Key West. Everything was in place for the final step in his carefully-thought-out plan.

He smiled to himself. No threats were left. Cassamayor was out of the picture. Martin Jones (A/K/A Moana) had skipped the country. Those two Ton-Ton hitmen had been shipped back to Haiti in leg-irons. And DMD had disappeared in a "helicopter accident," thanks to that wily Beach Parsons, Jr. A cut fuel line did the trick.

Fortunately, that redheaded Coast Guard officer and his twice-dead friend Lavon Perry weren't a part of this. The two sailors had stumbled into the middle of his scheme, nearly screwing it up. Thank all the Jesuit saints that he didn't have to ask Beach to deal with them. This close to success, riling the U.S. military was the last thing he needed to happen.

No more *saleté spéciale* would be exported from Haiti's *Vallée Mystérieuse*. Sister Gaylord Badger and those mail-order nuns of the Sisters of the Shriveled Penance had served their purpose. It was never Da Turtle's plan to mine the anti-aging minerals. He merely needed enough to prove their effectiveness when negotiating with the cosmetics industry. They would pay dearly to suppress a substance that could render their products obsolete.

Estee Lauder had already ponied up $40 million, deposited straight into his Swiss bank account. Maybelline had promised $25 million. Clinique was good for $15 mil.

Revlon made an offer of $1 billion for the mining rights, but that wasn't in the cards. The Ton-Ton Macoute would never tolerate that. The *saleté spéciale* had to be protected from the outside world. This was essential to Vodouism, the true religion of Haiti. The *bokors* used it to reanimate the dead, a feat essential to displaying their powers and maintaining control over their followers.

By "followers," that meant 90 percent of the Haitian population. Those who paid lip service to the Catholic Church were merely maintaining a façade to the outside world which frowned on the practice of Vodou. Fools!

Da Turtle was a happy man, knowing he would no longer be a "fixer" who worked for others. Betraying his partners, he had emerged as the head of this new cosmetic cartel. By the time the Health & Beauty Industry coughed up, he would have amassed a wealth approaching Bill Gates or Jeff Bezos – with much less effort than writing computer code or selling electronic books.

This called for a celebration.

He was sitting on his favorite stool in the Chart Room sipping a Papa's Pilar when a familiar voice said, "Did you forget about me, old chum?"

Da Turtle whirled around, coming face-to-face with Lord Pimlico Gorton Blackstraw. "You!" the terrapin exclaimed, realizing his oversight. He'd forgotten that DMD's straw-in-the-ear murder attempt had failed, causing the Lord a slight loss of hearing in his right ear, but no pain whatsoever.

"Yes me," the thin man acknowledged. He held a Walther PPK a few inches from Da Turtle's underbelly. "I think it's time we discussed business. I appreciate all your efforts, but I will be requiring that Swiss bank account number."

Da Turtle didn't move, remaining as still as a stone garden gnome. From the corner of his eye, he could see movement to the right of Lord Blackstraw, but his nemesis didn't hear the approaching danger due to his damaged ear.

Ka-bam!

Beach Parsons, Jr. fired his M1911 at close range, the .45 slug lodging in Lord Blackstraw's side, just below the ribs. But the man didn't flinch. He turned toward his assailant and muttered, "Son of a Beach!" as he returned fire.

Pow!

"Ouch, that hurts," said the mercenary, looking down at the blood on his shirt. The crimson was spreading like the opening of a rose's petals.

"Turnabout is fair play," stated Lord Blackstraw. "Want another?"

"No thanks," grunted the wounded Beach, "I'm going to need a drink." He picked up Da Turtle's glass of rum and downed it.

"Hey," muttered the man known to the Haitians as *Monsieur Tortue.* "That's my booze."

"Shut up, you double-crosser," ordered Lord Blackstraw, swinging his 9mm PPK to cover Da Turtle . "I want that bank number now."

"Do you plan to kill me?" asked his opponent, studying Lord Blackstraw with a beady reptilian eye.

"If I answered that question you might refuse to give me the number," reasoned the Lord. "So why not write it down on that cocktail napkin and take your chances."

"Not a very good bet," warned Beach Parsons, Jr., staunching the blood from the wound on his side. He grimaced as if suffering a toothache.

Da Turtle carefully examined the man in black who stood before him. No sign of damage from the .45 other than a ragged hole in his shirt. No blood, no outward pain. Was this man a zombie? "How are you not dead?" he asked, puzzled.

"I owe it to the very *saleté spéciale* that you are trying to steal. A spoonful in my tea each morning renders me impervious to pain, instills miraculous regenerative power, and fights aging. How old do you think I am, Jimmy?"

"I dunno," replied Da Turtle, "Sixty or seventy?"

"As a matter of fact, I'm two hundred and twelve. That dirt really works wonders."

"Regenerative powers? Got any on you?" Beach spoke up. "I could use a dose about now." He winced in pain. This wasn't the first time the mercenary had been shot, but it was never any fun.

"You'll live," snapped Lord Blackstraw. "I shot you through your love handles, old chum. A professional courtesy. I've always admired your work."

"Let's get past this little love fest and make a deal," interjected Da Turtle.

"Why make a deal when I can have it all?" the Lord smiled grimly. "I've never been fond of cold-blooded creatures."

"You're pretty cold-blooded yourself," replied the small man, a touch of admiration in his voice.

"Hi-ho," a voice interrupted the bar scene. "Who's buying the drinks?"

Everyone turned to see the Coast Guard officer known as *Le Grand Rouge*. He stood there like a redheaded Colossus of Rhodes, backed by half-a-dozen armed sailors.

Da Turtle said, "I'm buying if you will shoot this phony British Lord."

For a second no one moved, everyone in the bar as remained as stationary as a tableau in a department store window.

Then shots rang out, breaking bottles, splintering wood in the polished bar, ricocheting off walls. The smell of cordite filled the tiny room. Lord Pimlico Gorton Blackstraw had wounded Big Red and the sailors had returned fire. Da Turtle retreated to a strategic position behind the bar. And that Son of a Beach hunkered in a fetal position on the floor.

When all the shooting stopped, Da Turtle was surprised to see that Lord Blackstraw had disappeared like a stage magician, leaving behind nothing but a daemonic puff of smoke.

Damn!

Stepping out from behind the bullet-ridden bar where he had sought refuge during the affray, Da Turtle half expected to see the body of an old man, horribly wrinkled and disfigured, with a knife plunged into his heart. But a quick glance at the wreckage of the Chart Room Bar revealed that this had not been a theatrical exhibition of the denouement in Wilde's *The Portrait of Dorian Gray*. No knifed corpse, no undamaged painting of a handsome young Brit ... and no trace of the long-lived Lord.

"Well, it looks like that old British lord has finally gone on to his reward," Beach remarked after the smoke cleared. "But, maybe I shouldn't judge by appearances; anyone who could take a .45 slug in his belly without missing a beat might also have the power to make himself invisible."

Da Turtle replied in a knowing, world-weary tone, "My young friend, *it is only shallow people who do not judge by appearances. The true mystery of the world is the visible, not the invisible ...*" After pondering that enigmatic observation for a few seconds, Beach shrugged: "I'll have to defer to your experience on that." Reaching for one of the remaining unbroken bottles on the bar, Da Turtle refilled his glass and responded, like a teacher to a student, "*Experience is merely the name men gave to their mistakes.*" After pausing to take a sip of rum, he continued: "*You may fancy yourself safe and think yourself strong. But a chance tone of color in a room or a morning sky, a particular perfume that you had once loved and that brings subtle memories with it, a line from a forgotten*

99

poem that you had come across again, a cadence from a piece of music that you had ceased to play ... I tell you, that it is on things like these that our lives depend. "

Beach was puzzled by this philosophical musing from the taciturn lawyer, who might charitably be described as laconic, and less charitably as tight-lipped (if Turtles have lips,) Beach noted wryly to himself. So he nodded as if in agreement, while making an attempt to turn his employer's attention to more pressing matters – like getting the hell out of the Chart Room before the cops arrived.

"Well, I guess you're right boss, but as enlightening as it is, we'd better not waste time talking about that stuff and vamoose, pronto!"

Da Turtle knew that Cassamayor' s cohorts in blue, known to shoot first and ask questions later, would relish the chance to bag a big-name trophy; and there was no bigger in Key West than the circuitous lawyer. However, Da Turtle was in a reflective mood, and facilitated by a second shot of rum, wasn't quite ready to end this rare exercise in pedagogical discourse. Beach, *"If one doesn't talk about a thing, it has never happened. It is simply expression that gives reality to things."* Hearing the sound of approaching sirens, Beach exclaimed, "Boss, I don't know about all that, but I know the cops will be here in a skinny minute."

Raising his hooded non-blinking eyes to make a point, Da Turtle replied *"You know more than you think you know, just as you know less than you want to know."* Draining the last drops from his glass, the cynical solicitor continued, "So, don't concern yourself with what you don't know; *Knowledge would be fatal. It is the uncertainty that charms ..."*

With that, Da Turtle exited the wrecked bar moments before Key West's finest burst in. As he stealthily departed via a seldom-used back door of the Pier House, Da Turtle realized that, *"he wanted to be where no one would know who he was. He wanted to escape from himself.*

He felt that if he brooded on what he had gone through he would sicken or grow mad. There were sins whose

100

fascination was more in the memory than in the doing of them, strange triumphs that gratified the pride more than the passions, and gave to the intellect a quickened sense of joy ... But this was not one of them. It was a thing to be driven out of the mind, to be drugged with poppies, to be strangled lest it might strangle one itself."

Turning to his bodyguard, he declared, *"I am tired of myself tonight. I should like to be somebody else."*

Writer's acknowledgement: All italicized words are taken directly (if out of context) from Oscar Wilde's *The Portrait of Dorian Gray*

With those moving words the duo exited the smoldering remains of the Chart Room Bar. As they raced past the pool, the wily Turtle tore away his common garb to reveal a slinky, natural fiber, crenulated, strapless cocktail gown. It was indeed the classic, *Little Black Dress*.

Stunned beyond explanation or understanding, Beach clutched his side; it hurt badly, but he wasn't sure if it was from being shot, or from laughing like an idiot every time he looked at his boss. Beach moved forward with heightened senses, watching for danger, but avoiding eye contact with Da Turtle. This ambulation caused a painful crick to develop in Beach's neck as he walked awkwardly ahead. He'd never seen Da Turtle without his usual shell of drab shorts, absurd T-shirts, a too-small red Speedo swim suit that he wore as underwear and a series of ill-fitting, miss-matched flip flops. It was unnerving.

Finally, with no sign of pursuit, curiosity got the better of Beach. He needed a dose of adrenalin to keep his wits and always laughed hardest when things were the worst. He stopped and turned back to find Da Turtle drawing deep breaths and leaning against a dumpster behind, *Tootsie's Smokin' Squid Lounge*. The clever fellow had somehow managed to apply black face make up, a blonde wig and fluorescent lip stick while running for his life and now stood, ass up, elbow on a dumpster in a pair of Senna Onyx turtle-skin wingtip shoes with three inch lifts.

As Beach approached, Da Turtle grabbed a discarded

banana from the dumpster. It looked like a microphone when he held it to his rouged lips and began belting out an Al Jolson style chorus from the Village People's famous Y.M.C.A.

Da Turtle had undergone such a complete and rapid transformation even his own mother would not recognize him. He was, as people who knew him often remarked, a chameleon of the first water.

"As long as the ball is in the air, no one has won, no one has lost," Da Turtle said softly to Beach.

In Beach's opinion, Da Turtle had gone off the rails after being metaphorically flipped on his back by recent events. He gazed at his employer whose dark obsidian eyes unblinkingly sought Beach's understanding and also confirmed that which Beach had known all along... he was not going to get paid.

"Get some rest, Young Beach, I got it from here..." and with those few taciturn words Da Turtle smiled with freshly painted *faux* lips, then turned away down dark pungent alley on his journey toward the other side of sunrise. It would be an unsavory passage, dead-end trails, a booze scented maze engorged with unemployed writers and attorneys with hairy arm pits holding signs aloft, "Will talk for Money" "Will make up words for Money," Will think for Money," that type of thing . But, it was in the end, the alley of his dreams and the backstreet of his fate and, one fucking smart move, Beach was impressed. Da Turtle always seemed to come out on top. He was a floater.

Da Turtle got a new shell on!

The staccato pitter-patter of the small plates nailed onto the heels of Da Turtle 's wingtip shoes, which were said to prevent bow-leggedness, echoed distinctly off grimy street bricks each engraved with the name of a famously dead person and the rhythmic metallic tapping entertained an audience of open-mouthed, grinning green dumpsters. Bewildered bugs went blind and died in the brilliance of the halogen street lights as Beach turned upwind to look for a bar. He found three without moving his head sideways.

It was cool, dark and dank inside the Mostly Money Pub, a small establishment that promoted itself as, "A Dive for Divers," located just off Dung Beetle Lane. A mildewed black and white photograph of Johnny Weissmuller in drag hung unevenly above the cash register. Beach grabbed a bar stool and ordered a Key Deer beer. The stool was wet. A row of abandoned snorkels lined the bar above his head. Many had been made into one-use bongs and smelled strongly of ganja. The bar top was a stained and cracked mirror where a few patrons sat staring downwards, as if trying to find themselves in the depth of their own image.

While Beach waited for nourishment he continued to admire Da Turtle's uncanny ability to change his appearance in an instant. He'd gone into his shell as one person and come out another! The she-man, was an obvious survivor by nature and deed and need not worry about the cops, or anyone else, recognizing him now. Da Turtle had morphed into a *Da Turtlette* and was safe for the moment, at least in the soft underbelly of the all-forgiving island, and as for Beach Parsons; he might be out of a job. It was his own ass he had to worry about now.

~ ~ ~

I opened my eyes and tried to look around without attracting attention. It didn't work. As I moved my head I looked straight at the Son of a Beach. Not good. He was very much alive.

"Is Da Turtle gone?"

"Hope so." *Le Gran Rouge* looked around, no Turtle.

"Alright guys, it's over. Drinks are on the officer corps."

"Corpse is what I feel like," I said as I got up. The rest of the dead, wounded and pseudo-damaged were getting up on their feet.

"Hell of a performance" the bar tender said as he commenced to fill glasses. "All those rehearsals worked pretty well. Still, some real damage. Who plans on paying?"

"Put away your money, Lieutenant as the real corpse, I will certainly pay. Noblesse oblige," said Lord Blackstraw. "Coin of the realm or do you require payment of another

103

kind"?

We were all trying not to stare at the hole in his shoulder. No blood, just a round space.

The bartender also gaped and mumbled, "Payment in dollars is fine."

Blackstraw pulled a wad of cash from his waist coat, Some of them were big, and old enough be pre-WW1 gold deposit notes. "I SIMPLY Must be off," he said .

And I swear he disappeared before he went out the door. I looked at Beach. "A bit theatrical, but it did the job."

"One of my better," he replied. "Don't quit your day job. It took you half a minute to fall down. You looked like you were in a silent movie."

"Thank you, Mr. DeMille," I replied.

Blackstraw had actually come up with the kernel of a plan and Beach had filled in the details. Blackstraw needed to keep his secret – as he put it, "It was getting harder and harder to be, and stay, that old." He remained in Haiti because their public record keeping was so abominable. As he liked to say, "Once this wretched place becomes computerized, the next stop is Borkino Faso. But for now it must be borne, stiff upper lip and all that." Da Turtle would blow that particular whistle if and when it suited him. Ergo, either Da Turtle had to be convinced to go or he, Blackstraw, would have to. As the Turtle was proving to be so hard to kill, smoke and mirrors were called for. Next stop, the Beach.

Beach was tiring of his day job as a reptile's factotum. He wasn't getting any younger. Beech didn't want to be legit; he merely wanted to be comfortable. With Da Turtle, he never would be. He mentioned to Blackstraw that he, Beach, had been a technical advisor in a series of action movies – "Hired Killer" and its six pre-sequels. If he could stage something convincing, Da Turtle would go to ground thinking that his problems were over. As the other loose end, they contacted me. I had to come to a permanent end too. That, and with his protection out of the way, someone might just track him down. I signed on immediately. I brought a few of the crew along for local color. We rehearsed each night for a week after the bar had closed. Beach pronounced himself satisfied. Next night, we did it for real.

The police pulled up and weren't happy that the mayhem hadn't been real. Still, with a few drinks and a thousand dollars to split, they soon regained their sense of humor. Key West's finest at their heroic best.

Da Turtle had been listening to what he thought had been real shooting. He also saw the lights and heard the sirens. Wonderful, he thought to himself. He was humming, or as close to humming as a turtle can, "Send in the Clowns." Once again life imitates the theater. The clowns had indeed been sent for, and had dispatched themselves accordingly. He had surpassed himself yet again. Da Turtle kept walking toward his office. Being dark, he didn't notice a small cloud of acrid gas until he inhaled it. He became dizzy and started to fall.

Da Turtle woke up a few hours later, his nose was running and his feet smelled. Was he upside down? His head hurt and more disturbing, he was manacled to a cargo pallet in the back of a large, noisy airplane. He blinked his obsidian eyes and noticed a confident looking man seated across the way staring at him, like a fisherman staring at a perch.

"I'm a lawyer," Da Turtle bellowed, "I know my rights. I need food and water."

"I'm not a cop," Smith replied, "so I don't care about your rights and as far as food goes," Smith produced a bowl, a spoon and a BIC lighter. "I'm gonna make turtle soup, want some?"

Thank you for reading.
Please review this book. Reviews
help others find Absolutely Amazing eBooks and
inspire us to keep providing these marvelous tales.
If you would like to be put on our email list
to receive updates on new releases,
contests, and promotions, please go to
AbsolutelyAmazingEbooks.com and sign up.

AUTHORS PAGE
THE COMMITTEE

Andrew Daly: Born into an Army family that settled in Western Washington State and educated by taxpayer dollars, he immediately demonstrated his lack of character by leaving Washington and embarked on a career in the U.S. Coast Guard and other acronymic government agencies. He participated in Operation Haiti in 1983 and eventually washed ashore in the Florida Keys where he is consistently mistaken for a gentleman and scholar.

Dane M. Dastugue: Raised on a dairy farm in south Louisiana, DMD has survived, even after becoming a diligent student of the Classics, a Navy submariner, a fleet salvage and oil field diver and a corporate manager. He now spends his days vigorously attending to his pond, learning the ways of the opossum and debating the works of Thucydides with the family Poodle.

Jim "Da Turtle" Hendrick: National debate champion, formidable attorney and enemy of the hare, he fled the snow infested wastelands of New York and headed south. Eventually, Da Turtle ran out of road in the Florida Keys and set out to save the environment, or at least protect a small piece of it from over eager developers. Now serving as the resident Jedi Land Use Master of the Florida Keys, Jim inspires those around him to love when they can, laugh when they shouldn't, and always help a friend in need.

Mac McCausland: Navy (retired) Flag Chef (retired) Butcher, Baker and Candle stick maker, Sculptor, Painter and Costume maker, McCausland is 10 pounds of talent in a 5 pound bag. An all-around nice guy and friend of mankind, he avoids grey areas and hopes someday his cat will treat him with respect.

Shirrel Rhoades: A man of many hats, but only one suit, he is author of numerous mysteries and travel books, a publisher, syndicated film critic, former NYU professor, and museum president. And, if that's not enough, he originated the annual Key West Mystery Writers Festival. Known as the "Mother Teresa" of aspiring authors, he encourages all to do their best and walks his dog when necessary.

Reef Perkins: Born in the Wolverine state with an unnatural thirst for adventure, and a distinct lack of regard for parental advice, he joined the Army and later attended the Navy Salvage Officers School in Washington D.C. Upon graduation as a certified fool, he became a valuable military asset and, not surprisingly, was immediately shipped to Vietnam to ply his skills. An uncomfortable return to civilization could not be tolerated and he moved on to a life of high misadventure as an experimental diver, smuggler, perp, roofer and salvage master in Key West, Florida. Yes, he is still alive and has written the best-selling memoir, *Sex, Salvage and Secrets* published by *Absolutely Amazing eBooks*.

Special thanks to Commander Mac McCausland, CRN for devoting his extraordinary artistic talent to designing and creating the cover of this book.